STORM HOUND

Books by Claire Fayers

The Accidental Pirates:
Voyage to Magical North
Journey to Dragon Island

Mirror Magic

STORM HOUND

CLAIRE FAYERS

MACMILLAN CHILDREN'S BOOKS

First published 2019 by Macmillan Children's Books
an imprint of Pan Macmillan
20 New Wharf Road, London N1 9RR
Associated companies throughout the world
www.panmacmillan.com

ISBN 978-1-5098-9504-5

The author wishes to acknowledge the award of a Literature Wales
Writer's Bursary supported by the National Lottery through
Arts Council of Wales for the purpose of completing this novel.

1 3 5 7 9 8 6 4 2

A CIP catalogue record for this book is available from
the British Library.

Printed and bound by CPI Group (UK) Ltd, Croydon CR0 4YY

To my cats. I'm so sorry.
I have no idea how this book happened.

CHAPTER 1

He was Storm of Odin, last-born hound of the Wild Hunt that runs across the plains of the sky on stormy nights. He was barely four months old, but almost as tall as the crimson-tailed horses that raced before him. His coat was the black of the deepest midnight; his eyes shone golden-bright, alive with excitement.

He was Storm of Odin and this was his first hunt. He opened his mouth and howled, his voice joining the cries of the pack around him. The scream of hunting horns echoed between the wide horizons, and moonlight glanced off the hunters' helmets and the tips of their spears. Sky and earth trembled together.

He was Storm of Odin, and . . .

. . . he was having a little trouble keeping up.

He ran as fast as ever – faster, in fact, because he was straining now, his muscles beginning to ache, and the wild joy of the hunt was being overtaken by an uneasy feeling that all was not well. He dropped his head and his howls became a series of pants and grunts as he struggled to keep his legs moving forward. The crimson horsetails were no longer in his face but flickered in the darkness ahead.

The stormhound slowed, and his paws began to sink through the cloud beneath him. He howled again, his voice less like thunder across cloud-topped mountains and more a cry of: 'Hey, wait for me!'

No one heard. No one waited.

The Wild Hunt rushed on.

Far behind them all, Storm of Odin uttered a final yelp and fell from the sky.

Morning came and brought a headache with it. The sunlight made everything bright and sharp-edged – much bigger than he'd expected. The sky, no longer thunder-filled, was a clear, light grey, speckled with white wisps that didn't deserve the name of clouds. Mountains rose in indistinct humps all around while, closer by, trees towered over him, their branches hung with faded green leaves. Grass pricked at his paws as he took his first step.

Where was he?

The only creatures in sight were a huddle of sheep staring at him from a field on the other side of a grey stripe on the ground. A road – he'd heard the huntsmen speak of them. Humans built them because they didn't have wild horses to carry them. Instead, they crawled along these grey paths in armoured shells like snails.

The stormhound stepped on to the road to look about. The surface was rough, surprisingly hard and smelled of warm stones and tar. A large sign stood opposite.

Y Fenni   5
Abergavenny   5

These shapes meant nothing to him. And why weren't the sheep fleeing from him in terror, or falling at his feet in awe? Were they so stupid they didn't know who he was?

Hey! Sheep! the stormhound shouted.

The sheep gazed blankly at him, chewing grass. Eventually, one of them wandered closer. *You talking to us?*

Who else would I be talking to? A growl rose in Storm of Odin's throat as he prowled forward. *I am Storm of Odin of the Wild Hunt. Did you not hear us pass by last night?*

The sheep looked at one another and back at him. *If you're a stormhound,* said the one who'd spoken before, *I'm Aries. The Ram – get it?*

And I'm Rameses of Egypt, another one baaed. The whole flock fell about laughing.

Storm of Odin growled again in annoyance. *You're not even rams, you stupid sheep.*

The sheep only laughed harder.

Caaaaaaar! one of them shouted.

The stormhound shook his head. *Don't you mean 'baaaaa'?*

The ground trembled. Storm of Odin leaped backwards just in time. A rush of air, a noise like thunder and something metal roared by on the road. It was vast – the size of a chariot – and almost as loud as the Wild Hunt.

A moment later it was gone.

The stormhound rolled over and came up coughing. The air tasted of smoke and oil.

Car, the sheep said smugly. The rest of the flock chewed grass frantically, looking as if they were trying not to laugh.

Another of the metal things rushed into sight and shot by, faster and noisier than anything the stormhound had seen in his short life.

What do you get if you cross a stormhound and a sheep? one of the sheep asked. *A very baaaaaaad dog. Go back to the sky, storm puppy. It's not safe here.*

Storm puppy? Storm of Odin growled at the insult. He put a paw on the road, intending to cross over and teach the sheep a lesson, but he felt another rumble begin to build and stepped back. Odin would smite the sheep for their insolence when the Hunt returned. He turned his back with as much dignity as he could muster and began to walk.

He was much slower than last night. The thorny weeds at the side of the road stung his paws and every time a metal car came past the wind buffeted him and he had to flatten himself to the ground. After a while, rain began to fall and he plodded on through puddles. He wanted to sit down and rest but forced himself on. This grey road must lead somewhere – why else would the humans rush along it in such a hurry?

Then, unexpectedly, a car swerved to the side of the road and stopped. A door opened and a man stepped out.

Storm of Odin began to growl and stopped in surprise. The man was huge, so tall that his face was a faraway blur. The stormhound scuttled backwards on his bottom. This was far worse than he'd thought. He hadn't fallen into the world of men, after all, but a land of giants!

The giant squatted and stretched out a hand, palm down. 'It's all right.'

No, it wasn't all right. It was very *not* all right. The human world was not supposed to be this big.

Unless . . .

Oh no.

The thought had been knocking quietly for his attention for some time, but Storm of Odin hadn't wanted to let it in. Now, it overwhelmed him. He looked down at the earth, at his two front paws, glossy black and quite small in the grass. He felt one of his ears flop sideways and though he growled with effort he couldn't make it stand up again.

The man was not a giant. Storm of Odin was small. This world had shrunk him. He let out a whimper of despair.

The man lifted him out of the grass with hands that smelled of mint and soap. Storm of Odin bared his teeth.

You're a fierce little thing, aren't you?' the man said, and ruffled the stormhound's black ears.

This was worse humiliation than anything so far. When the great Lord Odin got to hear about this, he would smite this man and his tin shell from the face of the earth.

'What kind of person would abandon a puppy?' the man asked.

The Wild Hunt, that's who. But it wasn't their fault I got left behind, and they'll be back soon, so if you would kindly release me and be on your way I will consider asking Odin not to blast your home and family with thundery vengeance.

The man clearly didn't understand a word. Instead of putting Storm of Odin down on the ground, he carried him to the car and placed him gently on the back seat. Then he produced a blanket and proceeded to dry the stormhound's wet coat.

A fluffy blanket. Pink, printed all over with kittens and smelling of cat.

This was too much. Storm of Odin shook himself free and stood up, ready to enact his own thundery vengeance here and now, but the man had already let him go and was climbing into the front seat of the car.

'Hold tight, little guy,' he said.

Little guy? Eat lightning, human!

The metal shell rumbled and lurched. The stormhound's stomach lurched with it. On second thoughts, he'd just lie here and chew the man's blanket for a while. That'd teach him.

CHAPTER 2

Storm of Odin must have dozed off because he awoke to the sound of more human voices and someone lifting him away from the smelly blanket. He'd become quite attached to its damp edges and he scrabbled to keep hold of it. He might as well have saved his strength, because the man untangled the pink folds from his claws quite easily and held him, one-handed – a feat even Odin would not have managed. Storm froze in surprise for a second before he remembered his humiliating smallness. He let his ears flop down over his eyes, blotting out this horrible world. *The Wild Hunt would have returned to Odin's halls by now*. He imagined the feasting, the bones and scraps of meat thrown on the floor for the hounds to fight over, and his stomach ached.

'I found him at the side of Ross Road,' the man said. 'It looks like someone abandoned him there. I'd take him home but I have cats.'

A lover of cats – the enemy of hounds. No wonder the man wanted to imprison him. Storm of Odin lifted one ear a fraction and saw a second human peering down at him, a female human this time. She had sensibly chosen to protect her eyes with round pieces of glass held in a scarlet frame, although her clothing was just as flimsy as the man's. Her dress ended at her knees and her top half was swathed in a fuzzy thing that looked like it had been borrowed from a sheep, but, smelled overwhelmingly of dogs.

Storm of Odin stopped struggling. *You smell better, Fuzzy-Lady. I will allow you to approach. But be respectful.*

The Fuzzy-Lady stroked his head. 'He can't be more than a few months old. Poor little thing.'

He was not a poor little thing. He was a stormhound. He lived in the halls of Annwn beyond the mortal world. He hunted lightning for sport. He flattened his ears and gave a growl that should have sent clouds fleeing.

The Fuzzy-Lady smiled. 'He's a fighter, isn't he?'

Of course I'm a fighter. I am a hound of the Wild Hunt.

The Wild Hunt, which had run off and left him, he remembered. They hadn't even noticed when he fell from the sky. Storm of Odin shook his head and sneezed. It mattered not; they would find him soon enough. His stomach rumbled. He wondered if they had any food in this place.

*

Yes, there was food. Storm of Odin smelled it as the Fuzzy-Lady carried him through a doorway into a bright corridor. There were also dogs. Twenty or so of them, all lying in cells, separated by wire mesh.

A prison! Storm of Odin barked and yelped, but somehow Fuzzy-Lady held him so that he couldn't scrabble free. She opened the door of an empty cell.

'In you go,' she said, pushing him inside. She put a bowl of meaty chunks in front of him, patted his head and withdrew, locking his cell door firmly behind her.

Last night, Storm of Odin would have torn the wire mesh apart and chewed the pieces just for the fun of it. Right now, he was tired and hungry and his paws still ached from all the walking. He sniffed at the meaty chunks, then licked the gravy. It was surprisingly tasty and the chunks themselves were bite-sized with just the right amount of chewiness. This huge bowl all to himself was an unexpected luxury and he buried his nose in it.

The surrounding dogs watched curiously through their wire screens. After a while, he felt their gazes on him and he lifted his head from his bowl.

I am Storm of Odin, he said, *Stormhound of the Wild Hunt, follower of Odin One-Eye, also known as Arawn of the Otherworld. I run with thunder and lighting and all creatures tremble when I pass.* He bowed his head a little to show that none of them needed to fear him. He had no quarrel with these dogs. They were prisoners here the same as him and he would treat them kindly. *What is this place?* he asked.

None of the dogs appeared very impressed.

We're in the home for homeless dogs, dear, an old female in the cell next to his said. *You don't need to worry. We live here until a new human comes to choose us. You should get some sleep. You've had a hard morning.*

Storm of Odin felt his coat bristle. *On the contrary, I have had a hard night. I ran with the Wild Hunt through the sky above the world of men. We passed over plains, oceans and mountains.*

You have gravy on your nose, the old dog said.

The stormhound licked it clean irritably. *You're not listening. We chased lightning bolts across the midnight sky, I'll have you know.*

I don't see any Wild Hunt, another voice said. *What are you doing here? On holiday, are you?*

Storm of Odin turned to see a white terrier with bright eyes and ears like triangles. The terrier cocked his head on one side and grinned, his tongue poking out. *You don't look like a stormhound. I thought the Hounds of Annwn were white with red ears.*

The stormhound growled at his impertinence. *Some are. And some of us are black as midnight. Stormhounds don't all look the same, you know.*

You have to admit, you are a bit small for a

11

stormhound, the lady dog said.

He should *be bigger*, Storm of Odin thought. He recalled the moment he'd begun to fall, that awful lurching feeling as the clouds gave way beneath his feet. The other hounds and the horses running on, none of them hearing his call for help. Shame squashed the breath out of him. He'd thought he was ready to join the Hunt. He'd wrestled with the other hounds to show how brave he was and he'd almost exploded with pride last night when Odin had whistled to him as the pack gathered. What would Odin think of him now?

In a moment, shame turned to anger – at himself for failing, and at the rest of the Hunt for leaving him. They should have noticed sooner. They should have slowed. The stormhound growled and his shadow flooded the floor of his cell, turning huge and black, filling the space with the scent of thunder.

The other dogs believed him then. They shrank back from him, the air suddenly sharp with their fear. The white terrier gave a nervous bark and lay down with his paws over his nose.

Storm of Odin watched, his puppy tail waving in satisfaction but as the last dog turned away from him, his satisfaction faded and turned into something new – a strange emptiness that felt almost like hunger, except he'd only just eaten.

He'd never been so completely on his own before.

There had always been others – his mother and older siblings, and then, as he grew, the pack itself. His shadow shrank back around him and he curled up in the middle of his cell, his tail twitching back and forth across his nose.

He was Storm of Odin and he was lonely.

CHAPTER 3

Jessie didn't want a dog – not any more.

She *had* wanted a puppy for as long as she could remember, right up until a few months ago. She'd filled a whole sketchbook with drawings. Big dogs with watchful expressions, little dogs that ran when she flicked through the corners of all the pages. Her dog would be small enough to curl up on her lap. A terrier, maybe, with bristly, white fur, triangular ears and a cheeky stare.

But their London flat had been too small for pets and Mum was allergic anyway so Jessie had made do with drawing – not that she'd done much of that in the past few months, either.

'Wake up, Lightning Bug,' Dad said. He and Ben were already scrambling out of the car.

Jessie sighed. She knew why Dad was doing this – he thought a puppy would make her happy – but he was wrong. A puppy would just remind her that he and Mum weren't married any more, that Mum was back in London, living in an even smaller flat, while

Jessie and Ben had moved to Wales with Dad for his job.

It made sense, Mum and Dad kept saying, and Jessie repeated it to herself now. Dad could afford a bigger house. They'd always planned to move out of London one day anyway. Mum would visit them here.

And, now that they didn't have to worry about allergies and space, here Jessie was, with Dad and Ben at the Abergavenny Dog Rescue Centre.

Jessie got out of the car and stood, pretending she was an artist surveying the scene. The past few nights had been stormy – the lightning had come back to get her, Dad had joked – but now the sun had broken through the clouds and dark humps of mountains slouched in the distance. Everything around them looked strange – too much grass, too much sky. She felt exposed here, as if anything might happen, and she didn't like it.

They'd only come to Wales once before, further north for a holiday when Ben was a baby, and it had been stormy then too. Jessie had got out of the house and had almost been struck by lightning. She didn't remember it at all – why would she when she'd only been four years old? She only knew about it now because Dad always went on about it.

Ben caught her hand, swinging on her arm. 'Jessie, come on!'

Dad smiled at them both, but the look in his eyes

was strained. Jessie squeezed Ben's hand before pulling away. She'd tell him she needed time to make up her mind and then she'd let the days go by without deciding until he'd forgotten all about owning a dog.

Ben grinned up at her.

'Lead on, Lightning Bug,' Dad said.

A lady wearing red glasses and the most hideous fuzzy blue cardigan Jessie had ever seen looked up from her desk as they opened the door.

'Hello,' she said. Her Welsh accent made her voice go up and down like music. 'I'm Seren. You must be the Price family.'

Not quite, Jessie thought, because the Price family included Mum. She looked around the room – old armchairs, two vases of wilting pink flowers on the window sill, and one of those pictures made up of dots that turn into something if you stare for long enough – a castle in this case.

Dad nudged her aside and held out his hand. 'I'm Stephen Price. These are my children, Ben and Jessie.'

'Jessie's wanted a dog forever,' Ben said.

'Has she?' Seren turned her gaze on Jessie. 'This is a small shelter and I take very good care of my dogs – my guests, I like to think. I only let them go to loving homes.'

Had she guessed Jessie was wasting her time? Jessie felt her cheeks grow hot and she stared at the carpet. Dad patted her on the shoulder. 'We're still settling in here,' he said. 'We moved a couple of weeks ago. We've almost got the house sorted now and, as Ben said, Jessie's always wanted a dog, so . . .'

He tailed off.

Seren stared at Jessie a moment longer. 'I always say that people don't choose dogs,' she said at last. 'Dogs choose people.' She smiled. 'Would you like to come and meet them?'

She took a bunch of keys from her desk and unlocked the door behind her. The sound of yapping filled the air.

Ben cheered and rushed in.

'I can see your brother is a true dog-lover,' Seren said, a note of approval in her voice. Jessie didn't bother to correct her. She took a step after Ben and paused. A row of pens stretched down either side of a corridor. She looked round and saw a fat, brown dog gazing up at her from the first pen, his tail thumping on the floor. Next door to him, a sandy Labrador got up and stretched. Jessie felt something stir inside her and she looked away quickly.

'What happens to them if no one chooses them?' she asked.

Seren bent to scratch the Labrador's head through the wire. 'They live here and I look after them. They'd all like to be settled with new families, but this is the next best thing. Most of them do go

17

to new homes sooner or later.'

That made Jessie feel a bit better about leaving them all here.

The fat brown dog gave her a final pleading look and lay down.

'Dad,' Jessie said, 'I don't think . . .' She wasn't sure what to say next. She had to say something, though, before everyone started assuming they'd take a dog home.

Then Ben shouted, 'Jessie, come and look! I've found your dog.'

Jessie's heart dropped. Ben ran back to her and grabbed her hand, tugging her on down the corridor, past various dogs who watched her curiously.

'Here!' Ben announced.

Jessie's breath caught in her throat. A small, white terrier gazed up at her through the wire mesh. He had cheeky eyes, a pink tongue that lolled out of the side of his mouth and little ears standing up in triangles amid tufts of wiry hair. He looked like he was laughing and for one moment, before she squashed the feeling, Jessie wanted to laugh too.

This was the dog she'd drawn running in the corner of her sketchpad. It was the dog she'd always dreamed of owning.

Dad touched her shoulder. 'Jessie?'

Jessie held her breath for a second. All she had to say was 'yes' and they'd take the dog home. She'd look after him and they'd go on walks and play together, and in the nights he'd curl up on her feet and sleep.

'No,' Jessie said.

Her voice shook.

Ben let go of her hand, his face falling. 'But why? This is the exactly right dog.'

Jessie turned her back on the pen so she wouldn't have to see the cheeky eyes watching her. 'I'm sorry, Ben. Dad, can we go?'

'If you like,' he said. 'Maybe this was too soon.'

Then Jessie saw something move in the pen opposite her. It seemed darker than the others, full of shadow even though there was a light on in the ceiling right above. She walked closer, curious.

'He came in two days ago,' Seren said. 'Someone found him walking along the side of the road – abandoned, we think. I've asked around and no one seems to be looking for him.'

Jessie's gaze followed the shadow back. It stretched from the empty food bowl at the front of the pen all the way to a small, black puppy who crouched at the far end, his eyes fixed on Jessie's face.

She knew it was a 'he' without asking. He had one upright ear, and one that flopped over, almost covering his left eye. Jessie took another step forward and the puppy let out a growl like a miniature roll of thunder.

Jessie felt something turn over in her stomach. She

crouched lower, then sat on the floor in front of the pen, peering in. The little dog snarled at her, but he didn't seem to mean it. There was something lost and bewildered in his gaze as he sat, eclipsed by shadow, as if he were wondering how exactly he'd ended up in this place.

'Hello,' Jessie said softly. 'I know exactly how you feel.'

Ben swung on her shoulder. 'Jessie, come on, let's get the white dog.'

'I get to choose, Ben,' she said, surprising herself. She wiggled her fingers through the mesh. The puppy's snarl turned into a whine and he lowered his head and crept to the wire to sniff the tips of her fingers. Apparently satisfied, he sat down and fixed her with a stare that swallowed her whole.

'Jessie, you always said you wanted a small white dog,' Dad said. 'The terrier looks friendly.'

Jessie swept her hair back out of her eyes. 'That was before.' Her voice crackled. He was the opposite of the dog she wanted, but somehow, she didn't know why, that felt right. She stood up and turned to face Seren. 'You said dogs choose people. He's just chosen me.'

Seren fiddled with her glasses. 'He's got to go to the vet this evening. And we don't know for sure he's been abandoned. Someone might still claim him.'

'Then we'll wait,' Jessie said. 'Ben, what do you think?'

'I suppose.' Ben looked doubtful, then he grinned. 'All right, I'm going to choose his name, though. I vote for Floppy – look at his ear.'

The puppy gave Ben a look that said, *Call me Floppy one more time and I'll eat you.*

Jessie shook her head and sat back, gazing at the puppy, from his deep brown eyes to his paws, which seemed twice as big as they needed to be. 'He's as dark as a storm cloud,' she said at last. 'I'm going to call him Storm.'

The puppy cocked his head as if thinking about it, then he thumped his tail in approval and stood up to fix Seren with a hard, commanding stare. Seren's face melted into a smile.

'He is sweet, isn't he? All right, then. I shouldn't really do this, but I'll come round and visit your house this afternoon and we can fill out all the forms, then once he gets the all-clear from the vet you can take him. But if anyone claims him within the next month you'll have to give him back.'

Jessie nodded, only half listening. She scratched the puppy's head through the wire mesh.

'Hello, Storm,' she said.

CHAPTER 4

On a hill just outside Abergavenny, the number of sheep had more than doubled over the past couple of days. They took it in turns to stand in twos and threes and watch the road with expectant expressions. Or as close to expectant as any sheep can manage.

This afternoon, more than twenty sheep were grazing quietly when a silver car purred to a halt at the side of Ross Road, just by the sign that said: *Abergavenny 5*.

Three men got out. They all looked quite identical – to a sheep, anyway.

The first was tall and thin with grey hair the texture of wool caught in a bush. He stood gazing up and down the road, his hands in his pockets. One of his companions unfolded a map and laid it on the car bonnet. The third man produced a pair of metal sticks and began pacing up and down the grass slope by the road.

Several sheep strayed surreptitiously closer. The gentleman with the sticks paused mid-stride.

'I don't like the way the sheep are looking at us, Professor Utterby,' he said. 'They're up to something.'

The sheep all went back to eating grass.

The bush-haired gentleman sighed. Sometimes, he thought, life would be far easier without the assistance of his two colleagues. 'They're sheep,' he said. 'Brains made of wool. Ignore them.' He rummaged in his overcoat for a pocket-watch. It was getting on for four o'clock – yet another day wasted. If Nuffield hadn't miscalculated with his maps, if Ryston had been faster with his divining rods, they could have wrapped this up already.

A lorry roared by, making all three of them jump. Ryston scratched his head with one of his divining rods. Always slightly red-faced, his cheeks turned crimson.

Utterby walked up the slope to join him. 'If we could have a little quiet, it would help. Professor Nuffield, would you please stop shaking that map? You're not going to shake the location of the stormhound out of it.'

'I did with the manticore,' Nuffield said. He huffed into his moustache. 'You're welcome to continue the quest without me if you wish. Ryston is doing *such* a splendid job with those divining rods.'

Utterby ignored him. Nuffield might complain, but he would never walk out on a quest – especially not one as important as this. He snapped his watch shut.

'This is the site of the fall. I'm sure of it.'

'Then where is the stormhound?' Nuffield asked, jabbing at the map with two fingers.

A van drove by, too fast and far too close, blaring its horn. Utterby picked up a handful of dust from the ground and threw it in its wake. He smiled as he watched the van swerve. Inside the van, the driver let out a stream of very bad words as he noticed his trousers had suddenly and inexplicably vanished.

Professor Ryston's divining rods swung full circle. They might have just been picking up the surge of magic from Utterby, but they kept turning.

'Bingo,' Ryston said.

He pointed to a shallow, circular dent in the ground. 'This is where it landed.'

Utterby quelled his excitement. Finding the landing site was a good start, but only a start. He frowned as he watched Ryston's divining rods continue to spin. Thanks to him and Nuffield, they were days behind the creature. He turned to look at the sheep. Maybe they'd seen something. He could ask them with the right spell, but it would take an hour to prepare, and sheep were so stupid he doubted they'd remember even something as dramatic as a giant hound falling from the sky.

'There have been no reports of a hound terrorizing livestock and people around here,' he said. 'Yet a hound that size must eat.'

'It may be travelling at night,' Nuffield said. 'It could be miles away by now. And it might not be that big – we have no idea what these hounds really look like. It could be as small as a Great Dane, say.'

Professor Utterby shook his head. He'd spent the past two years studying the Hounds of Annwn. Giant beasts, some as black as midnight, others white with red ears, ten times the size of any mortal dog. And each one full of magic from their paws to the tips of their ears.

'The creature won't have gone far,' he said. 'Separated from its pack, it won't know what to do. It will probably hide close by, waiting for the Hunt to come back.' He looked up at the road sign. 'We're only five miles from Abergavenny. Let's start the search there.'

He climbed back into the driver's seat and waited while Nuffield and Ryston argued over who would go in the back. Utterby glowered at them both in the rear-view mirror. *Just like a pair of schoolchildren.* Still, once they had their hands on the stormhound, all this would be worth it.

For too long they'd got by with odd scraps of magic taken from the ancient elements of the mortal world.

Now they had the chance at something much bigger. The power of the Otherworld – the magic of Annwn. The hounds of the Wild Hunt were full of untamed power. A stormhound's tears, it was said, could heal any wound, its blood gave strength, its heart could be used in a hundred different dark rituals. And that was only the start.

The Otherworld really had no right to keep all that magic for itself while human magicians dwindled in number until there were only three of them left. And two were fairly useless, he thought, glancing at Nuffield and Ryston squabbling behind him. All that was about to change.

Professor Utterby began to hum. They would find the stormhound – find it, dissect it and use every part of it. With their new-found power, they would revive the ancient Invisible College and its research into the dark arts. They'd recruit more students, maybe even establish their own building. Utterby could picture the statue of himself inside: *Professor Utterby, founder of the new Invisible College.* He might even allow Nuffield and Ryston to have statues – smaller ones, of course.

Yes, he thought. They would make magic great again.

CHAPTER 5

He was Storm of Odin and he was at the vet's.

He still wasn't entirely sure what a vet was, but current evidence suggested it was a lady who hated dogs and expressed that hatred in a happy, cooing voice as she poked and prodded him.

Why did humans have to talk so much, anyway? Dogs were content with somewhere warm to lie and a full belly, but humans seemed to have this need to be constantly making a noise. Maybe it was because their voices were so pathetic compared with the might of Odin's thunder, and they were forever trying to make up for their lack of power with the sheer volume of words that came out of their mouths.

It didn't help that the Fuzzy-Lady had buckled a leather strap round his neck and attached another length of leather to it. Reins were for horses, not for hounds who ran free through the night sky. But Fuzzy-Lady hadn't even noticed Storm's protests or, if she had, she'd taken no notice.

The vet also ignored him and forced his mouth

open to check his teeth.

I'll give you a closer look at those if you like.

'All seems fine,' the vet said, not knowing how narrowly she'd escaped being struck down with thundery wrath.

Of course all looks fine. I am an immortal stormhound who knows neither injury nor disease. Storm tried to scrabble off the table. Where was that human girl – the one with the lightning touch? She'd left him in his cell, promising to come back for him tomorrow, and it must surely be tomorrow by now. The hours stretched longer than evening shadows. Time felt bigger, too, when you were little, it appeared.

The vet finally stopped prodding and turned away. Storm lay down on the shiny table. He hoped the girl Jessie would come back soon; he liked her smell – thundery with a faint copper tang as if she had some secret magic buried deep inside her.

Something stung him like an arrow. Storm shot upright, barking furiously.

'All done,' the vet said cheerfully.

All done? the old lady dog enquired once Storm was back in his cell at the dog prison.

Storm of Odin sighed.

The old dog padded across her cell and lay down next to the wire, as close to Storm as she could get. *This is hard for you, isn't it? Don't worry – your new humans will come back for you in the morning and you'll be out of here.*

Her voice was soft and a little wistful. Storm curled his tail around his legs. He wasn't sure he wanted humans – new or old. He wanted to be back where he belonged.

I don't understand why you stay here, he said. *All they do is talk to you in silly voices and stick sharp things in you.*

The old dog's ears twitched. *How would we get out, and where would we go if we managed it? We're not all stormhounds, you know. At least we have shelter here, and food. No one bothers us.*

But you're prisoners, Storm of Odin protested.

Guests, dear. A long-term guest, in my case. Most of the others will be chosen by humans.

But not you? Storm couldn't imagine what it would be like to live in this prison forever. Cautiously he shifted round so he could sniff the older dog through the wire mesh.

In the halls of Annwn, he said, *you'd have to be a great warrior of a hound to live to old age. We are born fighting.*

Do you enjoy it? the old dog asked.

Storm drew back a little in surprise. No one had ever asked him that question – he'd never even thought to wonder about it. *Yes,* he replied slowly. *Yes, I suppose I do. I mean, I did. I was different then, of course. And it's all training for the Wild Hunt.* He heaved a sigh. *The Hunt makes everything else worthwhile. And now I've lost it.*

The old dog sighed too, making Storm feel ashamed of his own self-pity. The Hunt would return for him, but the old dog had nothing to look forward to at all.

How did you come here? he asked her.

My family moved away and left me. Some humans want younger dogs. She stood up, stretched and lay down again. *Don't you go feeling sorry for me, now. I have everything I need here.*

A tiny spark of defiance crept into her scent. She'd almost convinced herself she was content, but not completely.

Don't you want to run through the skies and chase thunderbolts? Storm asked.

The old dog considered and shook her head, but the tip of her tail twitched restlessly.

Sometimes, when I was a pup, she said, *I used to watch the storm clouds race across the Black Mountains and I wondered what it would be like to join the Wild Hunt. But I grew old and I left my dreams behind. Wishing the world were somehow different won't change anything. As long as I have food and warmth, I'm happy. And maybe, one day, a family will come here and choose me. That's what I dream of now.*

Storm stared at her, aghast. A pain formed in his chest and escaped from him as a whine. Life in this world was harder than he realized, when dreams were reduced to meals and a blanket.

It's not fair, the white terrier in the cell opposite growled. *Those humans were going to choose me until they saw you.*

A few of the others dogs yapped agreement.

Storm's coat bristled. He felt his shadow swelling again. He hadn't asked to come here. If it weren't for these mesh cages, he'd teach that terrier a lesson. Storm stood up, trying to make himself as large as possible.

I do not intend to stay in your world any long than I have to, he said. *Once I've rejoined the Hunt, the humans may come back for you.*

The old dog sighed.

The terrier sneezed and licked his nose. *You're fooling yourself. Do you really think the Wild Hunt will come back just for you?*

Of course it would. He belonged to the pack. Storm let out a rumbling growl.

They will come. Is the word of a stormhound not enough for you?

The white dog stared at him, unapologetic and unafraid.

Don't pay any attention, the lady dog advised. *Terriers are always causing trouble.*

Storm turned his head to look at her. Her coat was dull brown, flecked with grey, and she smelled so much of this place that if he closed his eyes he might not notice her at all. But there was still that tiny spark

31

that said she hadn't completely given in. Her dreams had faded, but she hadn't forgotten them.

I will show you the Hunt, he promised. *When they come for me, you will see them.*

The old dog lowered her head. *I think I should like that.* She didn't quite believe him, but she hoped. It made Storm feel better.

Later, he dreamed he was running with the Hunt and he outran all of them, but when he turned round they'd all gone and he was alone in the sky.

Weakling, the wind whispered. *Call yourself a stormhound? You can't even run.*

He woke sharply, wondering where he was, then he saw the wire cage surrounding him and the empty bowl, licked clean. A soft whine rose inside him.

I find these things happen for a reason, the old dog said, coming to her side of the wire. Storm shook his head until his ears flapped. What possible reason could there be for any of this?

Then the door opened at the far end of the corridor and Storm heard voices he recognized.

He barked in relief and his tail momentarily forgot it was attached to a stormhound and wagged like a puppy's.

'Storm!' Jessie ran to his cell and knelt down respectfully before him. She looked happier today. The thunder was still there in her eyes, but it was softer, as if the sun were peeking over the edge of a cloud.

Her brother reached past her head and shoved his fingers through the wire mesh. Storm sniffed them – a solid, reassuring scent of earth.

You can be my special servant, he promised the boy. *Not as special as Jessie, but I will request Odin not to strike you down when he comes for me.*

'Yappy little thing, isn't he?' the Dad said.

As for you, human, you'd better strap on your armour and prepare to fight, because when Odin comes I will tell him about your insults.

'He's excited,' Jessie said. 'Will he grow very big?'

As big as a horse. As big as one of your houses. Big enough to hunt the lightning.

'He's got big paws, so you never know,' the Fuzzy-Lady said. 'Size isn't everything, though. He's got a big personality.'

She unlocked the cell and let Storm out. Jessie scooped him up straight into her arms and kissed his head. It was a bit wet but Storm of Odin bore the indignity. Maybe she'd give him some more of those meaty chunks soon. He was surprised at how much food this small mortal body seemed to require.

But then the unthinkable happened. Jessie's father brought out a narrow strip of blue leather. Storm howled in protest as Jessie buckled the thing round his neck. Betrayed! Betrayed by a child. The nasty thing even had a little tag attached as if she were labelling him.

Jessie set him on the floor and attached a leash to the hideous collar. 'Come on, Storm,' she said, tugging at it.

This was beyond rudeness. The child expected him to get up and go with her? With this tether attached? Storm of Odin sat down and let out a soft growl.

Jessie's father looked uncertain, his scent changing, overlaid with nervousness. 'I don't want a dog that growls and snaps. What if he bites you?'

'He won't,' Jessie said. 'He's frightened. You'd be scared too if you were abandoned as a baby.' She picked Storm back up.

Good: she was learning.

Behind, the white terrier yapped jealously and the old lady dog lay down with a sigh.

I made you a promise, Storm said to her, looking at her over Jessie's shoulder. *You will see the Hunt. Stormhounds always keep their word*. He didn't know how he'd keep his promise yet, but he meant it, and the old dog wagged her tail at him. Satisfied, Storm settled in Jessie's arms, resting his head over her shoulder so he could keep an eye out for threats.

'See?' Jessie said. 'He's fine.'

'I run an obedience class every Wednesday,' the Fuzzy-Lady said. 'You should bring Storm along.'

Jessie's father nodded. 'Good idea.'

Yes, it was a good idea, Storm agreed. These humans ought to learn some obedience.

34

CHAPTER 6

'Here we are, Storm,' Jessie said as she led the way through the narrow door into the humans' house. 'Home.'

He was a guest here, Storm remembered, so he should mind his manners: the realm of Annwn had strict rules about hospitality. He didn't, therefore, lift his leg to mark his territory, though the furry blue stuff that covered the floor definitely deserved it. He sniffed along the wall.

You live here? Where's the rest of it?

Odin's halls were vast. Stone walls, stone floors strewn with animal hides. Storm could picture them now – the great fires that roared at either end, the long tables where the hunters feasted, throwing scraps to the dogs. And then the pack would flop down in a heap, black and white bodies tangled together, and they'd sleep.

But here there was barely enough room to chase a cat. The narrow hall – only just wide enough for Jessie, Ben and their Dad to crowd in together – had one flight of stairs leading up from it, covered in the same furry cloth. And three doors. Storm had to count them twice to be sure there weren't more. All three of them made of some flimsy wood-like material that didn't smell of trees at all. They'd probably break if he jumped at them too hard.

'Storm, don't jump at the doors,' Jessie said. She opened the nearest one. 'This is the front room.'

It was tiny, cluttered with boxes. The seats looked quite comfortable but as soon as Storm jumped up to test them, Jessie's Dad picked him up.

'Best keep him off the furniture,' he said, carrying him out.

Jessie opened the next door. 'Here's the back room,' she said, showing Storm a room that looked almost the same as the front room except that it had a small table. Jessie moved on to the final door. 'And this is the kitchen.'

Storm took in the sight of brown cupboards, a counter loaded with more boxes, table legs and a strange white cabinet that hummed softly. *Where's the roaring fire?* he asked. *And the venison roasting on a spit, and the sacks of grain and cats chasing stray mice?* It was cold for a kitchen too, mainly due to the floor being made of hard, shiny stuff that looked like polished stone, but felt a bit like walking on ice.

'Sit, Storm,' Ben said. 'I want to take your picture to send to Mum.'

Storm didn't have time to sit for a portrait. It would take hours and he wanted to explore. But Ben held up a small, rectangular device and a light flashed. Storm jumped back, barking in surprise. The humans laughed, even Jessie's Dad, who should have had more sense, being fully grown.

Threaten me with lightning again, and I'll eat you, Storm grumbled.

At least there were lots of things to explore. Storm nosed through a box on the floor, finding paper that crackled satisfyingly and a stack of plates that proved far too delicate to be stood on.

'Why don't you take him into the garden?' Jessie's Dad suggested, lifting him away from the broken plates. 'I'll clear this up and do some more unpacking.'

Didn't they have servants to clear up? Apparently not. Jessie's Dad fetched a brush and began sweeping. Storm pounced at the bristles – prickly but not dangerous. And then Ben opened the door and Storm saw the garden.

Daylight! Grass! And a tree – an oak, no less, its branches stretching up crookedly, trying to touch the clouds. Storm gave a happy *yap* and darted off outdoors.

This was more like it. Still a bit small compared to the vast forests and pastures of Annwn, but the grass sprang nicely under his paws. There was a strip of brown earth like a moat all the way round.

I wonder if that's where the humans bury their treasure, Storm thought, and went to investigate.

Ben said something about flower beds, which Storm ignored. The two humans sat on the back step and watched as he dug for treasure. He found a few plants and tossed them out of the way, then sat back, panting. He could see mountains from here: a low peak rising up in the distance, and three hills in front of it, which, if he squinted, looked a bit like the paw of a giant dog. He knew the mortal world was indifferent to the world of magic, but the sight cheered him a little, as if the landscape had made an effort to welcome him. Storm ran back to Jessie and pawed at her leg to get her attention.

Why are you sitting? We should go hunting in the mountains.

'I've sent the photo to Mum,' Ben said, looking at a small rectangle with a shiny front. 'She said she'll ring us in a minute.'

Who is this Mum-Person? Why isn't she here to greet me?

'He almost looks like he's trying to tell us something,' Jessie said.

Storm sighed.

A bell rang inside the house. Was that the dinner gong? Storm ran to the door hopefully. But, no, the sound had already stopped.

'Jessie, Ben, it's your mum,' Jessie's Dad called.

Jessie and Ben both jumped up and dashed past Storm into the house. Storm wondered whether to follow them, but he hadn't finished smelling the whole garden yet.

And then he heard a hiss behind him and turned to see a cat standing on the fence.

Storm ran to the middle of the garden. *Begone, foul enemy!*

The cat didn't move. A skinny tabby, fur thinning with age, she stared at him with faded green eyes.

This is my territory, dog. Don't go leaving your stink all over it.

Storm stopped still, not quite sure how to respond. The cats in Odin's halls would never dare to come near a stormhound, never mind address one in that impertinent fashion. But in the world of humans he and this cat were about the same size – and the cat had the advantage of claws.

The cat hissed, a sound that seemed to be made up of malice and icy wind. Storm stood up straight, his shadow spreading to swallow the grass. *I am Storm of Odin, stormhound of the Wild Hunt. How dare you speak to me like that?*

The cat watched his shadow spread and started to clean behind one ear with her paw. *Don't bother me, stormhound. I've watched the Wild Hunt pass by in the dead of night. It doesn't impress me.*

Storm's bottom hit the grass in surprise. *Are you*

sure we're talking about the same Wild Hunt? Odin's Hunt. The Hunt of Arawn. Hounds and horses from the Otherworld riding through storm clouds?

The cat stared at him through narrowed eyes. *I am a cat – descended from gods. I don't need to run in a pack and snap at lightning to feel important.*

This was beyond insolence. Storm tensed, his coat prickling. *I could chase you up that tree.*

The cat dismissed the oak tree with a flick of her whiskers. *Yes, you probably could. Maybe I'll let you, then I can sit in the branches and laugh as your humans scold you.*

Storm turned to look at Jessie who was standing just inside the back door of the house, something pressed to her ear. *She serves me*, he said. *Why would she scold me? And, anyway, you're a cat. Mortal dogs chase cats. It is the order of things.*

Yes, but for some reason humans don't tend to like it, the cat replied. *You have a lot to learn about being a puppy, young disciple.*

What is that supposed to mean?

In this world you have a lot to learn and I can teach you. For a start, you should keep your magic hidden. Most humans wouldn't know magic if it bit them, but there are still some who can sense the power of the Otherworld. You don't want to attract their attention.

Storm looked at his shadow on the grass and tried

to pull the edges of it back towards him. It didn't move.

Not like that, the cat said. *You need to imagine that you're an ordinary puppy.*

I am not an ordinary puppy, Storm objected. Still, his shadow shrank a little.

The cat stood up and arched her back. *Better. You learn fast.*

I'm not learning at all. I don't take orders from cats.

Chase me, then, and see what happens. Or I shall sit here on this fence in the sun and you can stay in the garden and play with your ball. Stormhound.

She put so much scorn into that last word that Storm felt a growl rise in his throat and turn into a fury of barking. The cat darted off the fence and streaked towards the tree.

Storm gave chase. He was Storm of Odin, on the heels of an arrogant animal who was about to discover the unwisdom of angering a stormhound.

The cat clawed up the tree trunk out of reach. Storm tried to follow and found that his useless paws refused to take flight. He crashed into the bottom of the tree trunk, barking in frustration as the cat laughed. Storm saw Jessie lower the thing from her ear.

I have cornered the cat, Storm barked. *Fetch her down so I may teach her a lesson.*

The next moment, a lady burst out of the house next door, hollering like a Valkyrie. Something hit

Storm on the back of the head. He spun round with a yelp of surprise. She'd thrown a slipper at him! It lay in the grass where it had bounced off his head. Storm pounced on the offending object, sinking his teeth into it and instantly regretting it when his mouth filled with fluff and the stink of old lady feet.

'Bad dog!' the Valkyrie-Lady yelled. 'Leave Nutmeg alone!'

Storm paused. *Nutmeg? Is that your name?*

It's what she calls me. The cat turned her head. *Look out – here comes your human.*

Storm looked in time to see a small whirlwind shoot out of the house.

The old Valkyrie-Lady swung round, her mouth falling open in surprise. Storm dropped the disgusting-tasting slipper and sat back, his tail thumping the grass. Jessie could have been a Valkyrie herself. Her lightning scent blazed to life, filling the garden.

The old woman waved her remaining slipper. 'You need to keep your dog under control. It's bad enough I've got to put up with children making a racket without dogs attacking my cat.'

Jessie's scent sharpened. 'Storm wasn't attacking your cat.'

I was, actually. But I wasn't going to hurt her. Did you see me almost climb the tree?

Jessie tossed the chewed slipper back over the

fence and scooped Storm up in her arms.

'You're a very rude little girl,' the old woman shouted.

'And you're a very rude lady,' Jess shot back.

Storm watched over her shoulder as the cat scrabbled down the tree and dashed across the garden to the fence. *That's right: run away. Well done, human servant. I will tell Odin of your faithfulness.*

Jessie carried Storm into the house and placed him on the cold floor. 'Storm, you can't go chasing people's cats. Mrs Williams already hates us.'

She wasn't angry at him, Storm knew, she was angry at the old woman, but even so it weighed heavier than Odin's wrath. His fury blazed and was gone in a moment, but Jessie's had disappointment at its core. It shouldn't matter to him – he was a hound of the Wild Hunt and far beyond the disappointments of mere mortals – but even so he put his head on his paws and whined.

Jessie bent to stroke his head. 'It's OK,' she said. 'Just don't do it again. I'm going back to talk to Mum.'

Her scent filled with the sharp salt of tears. This Mum-Person had upset her, Storm thought, and he felt his coat bristle. He followed Jessie back through the house.

'My turn,' Jessie told Ben, taking a black thing from him and putting it to her ear. 'Mum, did Ben tell you about the puppy? When are you coming to visit?'

I chased a cat up a tree, Storm told Ben, but of course he didn't understand.

'Good boy, Storm,' Jessie's Dad said.

He wasn't a good boy. He'd chased a cat, which was not allowed, and angered the Valkyrie-Lady next door. Storm thumped his tail on the floor uncertainly. He really didn't understand humans at all.

CHAPTER 7

At nine o'clock the following Tuesday morning, a silver car glided to a halt outside the Abergavenny Dog Rescue Centre. Professor Utterby sat and stared through the windscreen at the small building with its colourful sign. His head throbbed. Professors Ryston and Nuffield had argued over who was getting the best room at the hotel last night, and then over who ate the last piece of toast at breakfast.

Who cared about rooms and breakfast when they were on the verge of their greatest discovery? And why had Ryston's divining rods led them here, of all places? Professor Utterby unclipped his seat belt and got out of the car. At least the place was open today – he'd forgotten about the bank holiday. Why did people still have those? When he was in charge of things, he'd do away with any holidays that interrupted important work.

The small building didn't look promising but they'd found no other trace of the stormhound since last Thursday at the roadside. They might as well take a look around.

A woman looked up from a desk as Utterby opened the door. She wore a fluffy red cardigan covered in animal hair and oversized glasses in the same ghastly shade. Utterby considered turning them blue to see if she noticed, but he wasn't here to perform magic tricks.

'Good morning,' he said. 'My name is Professor Utterby and these are my colleagues, Professors Nuffield and Ryston. We are looking for a dog.'

'A big one,' Nuffield added.

The woman at the desk frowned with suspicion. 'I don't just give dogs out to anyone who walks in. You'll need to make an appointment, and then arrange a home visit. Where do you live?'

Ryston coughed. 'Can we hurry this up? This place is setting off my asthma.'

Utterby sighed and took an envelope of powdered chalk from his top pocket. He emptied the powder into his hand and blew it into the woman's face. Specks of it landed on her glasses. She started to stand, her mouth opening in protest, then her expression turned blank and she slid back into her chair.

'Young lady,' Professor Utterby said firmly, 'we are on the trail of a dog and, hard as it is to believe, the trail led us to this place.' He looked around and saw the door behind the desk. 'They are through there, I take it?'

The woman blinked several times as if she were

trying to stay awake. 'My name is Seren Granger. Welcome to Abergavenny Dog Rescue Centre. How may I help you? The dogs are in the kennels.' She held out a bunch of keys.

'Thank you,' Utterby said, taking them. 'Please do not move until we return.'

Ryston began to wheeze the moment Utterby opened the door.

'You two, stay here and watch Miss Granger,' Utterby said.

Dogs cowered away from him as he strode through the door. Professor Utterby carefully scattered handfuls of powder across each pen and examined the dogs one at a time. Two Labradors, several medium-sized mongrels, but nothing that matched the description of a stormhound.

Then he sensed something else – dog, amplified a thousand times over, and overlaid with the sharper smell of magic.

Utterby walked closer. It came from the end pen. It was down to a mere shadow, but he could tell it was different to the elemental magic he used. Something that didn't belong to this world.

He threw a handful of powder into the pen, and then another. An old dog in the next pen scrabbled back, whimpering. Utterby paid her no attention because, where the powder landed, a shadow formed – the vast and terrible outline of a giant dog.

Professor Utterby had seen many terrible things during his study of the dark arts, but even he suppressed a shiver. He turned round slowly. A white terrier in the opposite pen gazed at him with a terrified expression.

'The hound was here,' Utterby whispered.

Here? But why? The beast didn't appear to have attacked the dogs. Maybe it had been attracted by their scent. It might be looking for a new pack to be part of.

He strode back out, elbowing Nuffield and Ryston aside. 'You, Miss Granger, wake up.'

Seren Granger grunted and stirred in her chair.

'There was a dog here,' Utterby said. 'A big one. Where did it go?'

'A family . . . Children.' Her head slumped forward and she began to snore.

'Could the animal have been adopted?' Nuffield asked. 'If it was clever and it was looking for a place to hide, maybe it's posing as a mortal dog.'

'Are you serious? A stormhound?' Utterby sighed in frustration. 'This may take a little more work than I'd anticipated. The hound is cunning. Where do children congregate these days?' he asked.

Ryston poked Seren Granger, who snored even louder. 'Parks?' he suggested. 'Hospitals? Schools?'

'A school might work,' Nuffield said. 'We could be visiting teachers. It's a long time since I taught a class.' He sounded a little wistful.

'I don't think they teach our kind of lessons,' Utterby said. But he too felt a sudden nostalgia. Why not a school? They needed a reason to stay here or the locals might start wondering what they were doing, and it was always tiresome when people became suspicious.

'We shall return to the hotel,' Utterby said. 'Ryston, you'll look up the local schools. Nuffield, you and I shall scour the mountains – carefully. We know the stormhound is here, and it is probably hiding. We don't want to act in haste and frighten it away.' He brushed the chalk dust off the sleeping woman's glasses. 'Forget we were here.'

Some time later, long after the noise of the professor's car had faded, the sound of a lone engine broke the silence. A motorbike purred along the road and came to a gentle stop outside the animal shelter.

The bike was the orange of sunset and various black lines and squiggles crawled over its sides. They looked a bit like writing, but it was anyone's guess what they meant – not that anyone looked long enough to wonder. For some reason, when the bike had passed people in town, everyone glanced away and walked purposefully in the opposite direction as if they'd just remembered something important. Even though a large white hare, missing the tip of one ear, sat upright on the pillion.

The rider removed her helmet, revealing short, silver hair and an expression so stony it could have been cut from the Welsh hills.

'You can't go in looking like that,' she said.

The hare shrugged and jumped off the bike. A moment later it had vanished and a boy stood in its place. He still looked quite hare-like – short and sturdy with white-blond hair. The tip of his right ear was missing.

'Can't I wait here for you?' he asked, wrinkling his nose. 'You know I don't like dogs.'

'It will only take a minute. Come on.'

She strode across to the building and opened the door.

A woman was snoring gently, slumped in a chair. She jumped and opened her eyes as the door slammed.

'Welcome to Abergavenny Dog Rescue Centre. I'm Seren Granger, would you like an appointment?'

She said it all in one breath, with a big smile as if she'd been dreaming the words just before she'd woken.

'Why would we want to make an appointment when we're already here?' the silver-haired visitor asked. She set her motorbike helmet on the desk and pulled off her gloves. Her nails were painted dark green with little swirls of gold that seemed to shift and dance in the light. 'Listen carefully. Three men came here earlier today. One was old, one middle-aged and one was young. What did they want?'

Seren rubbed her hands over her face, dislodging her glasses. 'What time is it?' She blinked blearily, her expression becoming confused. 'I came in at eight to feed the dogs. Then I sat down for a minute, and then . . . Are you sure you don't want to make an appointment?'

'Quite sure,' said the visitor.

The boy jiggled behind her. 'I told you I smelled magic here.'

'Yes, you're very clever. Be quiet now.'

She turned her attention back to the woman at the desk and held one hand up, her fingers spread. The swirls on her nails twisted faster. 'Pay attention now and think. Three men. Professors, they call themselves. What were they looking for?'

Seren's face twisted with the effort of remembering. 'A family . . . Children. Something about children.' She smiled suddenly. 'Schools! They said they were looking at schools.' She slumped back, breathing fast.

'Try casting another spell on her,' the boy said, earning himself a frown. 'Just a suggestion.'

'Magic is not a toy, Morfran.'

'I never said it was,' the boy grumbled, but his companion ignored him, pulling her gloves back on and picking up her helmet.

'Go back to sleep,' she told Seren.

There was enough of the professors' dark magic still on her that Seren slumped back in her chair, her eyes closing again.

The two visitors made their way outside.

'Schools,' the woman said. 'Why would they be interested in schools? They're looking for something, I know, but what? We need to find out what they're up to.' She eyed the boy thoughtfully. 'You better have a normal-sounding name. You can be David again if you like – David Morfran. And I'll be your Auntie Ceridwen.'

'You *are* my Auntie Ceridwen,' the boy said. 'Sort of.' Then, as his 'aunt' continued to stare at him, his face fell. 'Oh no. Please tell me you're not thinking what I think you're thinking.'

'I certainly am,' she said. 'I'd hardly fit in at school, would I?'

An hour later Seren woke again, looked at the clock and jumped up. How had she managed to sleep through the entire morning? She'd come in at eight as usual, fed the dogs, sat down for a moment and . . . She stood up and stretched. Thank goodness nobody had come in and found her asleep like that.

CHAPTER 8

The weekend had been bright, but on Monday morning the sky swarmed with grey clouds and Jessie woke with her head full of thunder. She didn't often remember her dreams, but this morning was different – she'd been running through dark clouds with the moon overhead and all around her dogs had howled and barked. Black dogs like Storm, only much bigger, and white dogs with red ears and tails.

She'd dreamed of dogs because of Storm, of course. She couldn't believe they'd only had him just over a week – it felt like he'd been part of her life for months. She'd sketched her first picture of him yesterday – the first time she'd drawn anything since they'd moved to Wales. She hadn't quite got his ears right, but was quite proud of how it had come out.

She rolled over in bed and felt her sketchpad jutting out from under the pillow. Strange: she was sure she'd left it in her drawer. She opened it and saw that the last page was full of scribbles.

She got out of bed and opened the bedroom door.

'Ben, have you been drawing in my books?'

'No.' He poked his head out of the bathroom and grinned at her. He was wearing his new school uniform – dark grey, like the clouds. 'Are you taking Storm for a walk?' he asked. 'Can I come?'

'If you want.' She dressed, frowning. If Ben hadn't drawn in her book, who had? Could she have done it in her sleep? She looked at the page again. The thick, scrawled lines were nothing like her neat, lifelike drawings. At first glance they seemed like random scribbles, but when she kept looking they took on a pattern of rushing wind and lightning flashes. They made her feel restless, as if she'd been cooped up inside for too long.

She pushed the book aside. She needed to get outside, to *run*.

Downstairs, Storm jumped up, his tail wagging. Dad was already dressed for work and smiling as if he'd been practising the expression. 'So. New start today.' His smile faltered for a second. 'Are you sure you'll be all right going by yourself?'

'Of course I will,' Jessie said, though her stomach filled with dread. This was worse than when she'd started high school in London last year. Everyone had been new then, but now she was going straight into Year Eight where everyone else would already know each other.

But it was just as bad for Ben, she reminded herself, and Ben's school was in the opposite direction to hers so Dad couldn't go with both of them anyway.

Jessie fetched Storm's lead from the hook Dad had put up by the door. 'We'll take Storm for a walk first.'

'Don't be long,' Dad said. 'You don't want to be late.'

She'd rather not go at all, Jessie thought, but she didn't say so.

Storm seemed to realize something was different this morning. Every time they'd taken him out so far, he'd wanted to stop and examine everything, but today he trotted along the road, tugging at the lead and after only ten minutes he turned back in the direction of the house.

'It's like he knows,' Ben said.

Storm turned his head and gave him a stare. Ben laughed, then heaved a sigh. 'Do you want to go to school?'

'No, not really,' Jessie admitted. She twisted Storm's lead round her hand. 'But it'll be fine, you'll see.' She tried not to think about all her friends back in London, excited to see each other after the holidays. She probably wouldn't see them for ages. 'It'll be fine,' she repeated, walking faster. That was what Mum always said. Even if things looked bad, they usually worked out for the best in the end.

*

Jessie kept repeating those words all the way to school. *Everything works out for the best*. It made her feel a bit better until she caught sight of the school gates. She paused in the road, her stomach dropping to her feet.

A group of girls barged by, knocking Jessie's school bag off her shoulder. 'Sorry!' one of them called as they hurried past. Jessie bent to retrieve the bag, her hands shaking a little. She didn't belong here – she didn't *want* to belong here. She hadn't realized how small she'd feel here, and how alone.

She almost turned back, but then she heard the growl of a motorbike. She stepped behind a tree as a bike appeared. It was orange and covered with dark squiggles – some sort of writing or symbols. The rider wore an orange helmet, and someone much smaller clung on behind – someone in a school uniform.

The bike stopped. 'Do I really have to do this?' the passenger asked. He removed his helmet. A boy, about the same age as Jessie. His pale blond hair blew across his face as he climbed off the bike. 'I've never been to school,' the boy protested. 'I don't even know what they do there.'

Jessie drew further back behind the tree, watching. It looked like she wasn't the only one who didn't want to go to school today.

The bike rider took off her own helmet. She didn't look like the sort of person who'd go around on a motorbike. She was old, grey-haired, though she had earrings all up her left ear.

'They learn things,' she said. 'You never know, you might even enjoy it.'

She raised her helmet to put it back on, then paused as she spotted Jessie behind the tree. 'What are you staring at?'

'Nothing,' Jessie said quickly.

The woman's expression reminded Jessie of stone. 'You were looking at the bike,' she said.

'Um, yes. It's a nice bike. Very orange.'

'You shouldn't be looking at it,' the woman said. She stood up off the saddle. 'Who are you? Where are you from?'

The boy grabbed her arm. 'Don't cause a scene, Auntie Ceridwen. People will see.'

His aunt paused, then shook her head and sat back down. 'Keep an eye on her,' she muttered.

Why? What had she done? Jessie backed away and hurried through the school gates. What a strange woman.

'You're a little late,' a frazzled-looking lady said, pushing various sheets of paper at Jessie. 'Here's your timetable, and your welcome letter, and a letter about school lunches. And here's the list of the school rules. Mr Heron likes everyone to have a copy. Assembly will be starting any minute. You should go straight in. Along the corridor and through the double doors. You're in class number two. There's a new boy starting today too, so you won't be on your own.'

Jessie had lost track halfway through the stream of words. She smiled politely. Where had the strange boy gone? He should have been right behind her. She shuffled through the pieces of paper as she left the office. A list of school rules, a timetable, a map of the school, a letter from Mr Heron the headmaster with a blurry black-and-white photo of himself. He hoped Jessie would enjoy her time in Abergavenny High School, that she'd work hard, that she'd follow the school rules. Wear the correct uniform, don't drop litter, don't run in the corridors, do your homework on time.

Jessie's thoughts went back to Storm. It was the first time they'd left him alone in the house. It was only until lunchtime and Dad said he'd probably curl up and sleep, not even noticing they were gone, and Jessie hoped he was all right.

Stuffing the papers into her bag, Jessie followed a group of girls along the corridor and into a hall that was already almost full. She wriggled into a space at the back, earning a few curious looks from the people around her. Her heart beat harder than normal, making her feel a little giddy.

She'd only just sat down when a door opened at the front of the hall and a tall man came through.

'Good morning,' he said. *'Bore da.'* He pronounced the last bit 'bo-ruh daa'. 'For visitors, that means "Good morning" in Welsh. I am Mr Heron, the headteacher of Abergavenny High School.'

He didn't look too bad. Would she have to learn Welsh? Jessie hadn't thought about that.

To her relief, Mr Heron continued in English. 'I'm pleased to welcome some important people to the school today.'

He meant her, didn't he? Jessie sank lower, hoping he hadn't seen her. Where was the new boy? She caught a flash of white-blond hair across the hall. She tensed, waiting for Mr Heron to ask them both to stand up. Instead, he walked back to the door at the side of the hall and opened it wide.

A low whispering ran through the hall as three men came in.

The first man was the tallest, and the oldest. His hair was a grey bush and he walked a little stiffly, possibly because he was wearing a very tight brown suit. Following him came a short, plump man with a bristling yellow moustache. And, at the rear, a much younger man, younger than Dad. He wore light blue jeans and a pink sweater with a rabbit on the front. A couple of the girls around Jessie giggled.

'I'd like you to welcome Professor Utterby, Professor Nuffield and Professor Ryston,' Mr Heron said, indicating the three men in turn. 'They are in

Abergavenny on secondment from . . .'

He paused, frowning, as if he'd momentarily forgotten what he was supposed to say. Something caught the light as Professor Ryston walked – a piece of metal jutting out of his pocket. Jessie sat up straighter, trying to see what it was.

'Bangor University,' Professor Utterby said. 'We are from Bangor University in North Wales and we are on special secondment to your area as part of . . . um . . . as part of the schools and universities special secondment scheme.'

Jessie had never heard of a secondment scheme. They'd never had any visiting professors in London. She could imagine Dad's voice when she told him about it later: *See? There are advantages to living here.*

One of the metal pieces fell from Professor Ryston's pocket with a clang. He scooped it up. Two boys in the front row laughed and stopped abruptly as Professor Utterby turned to glare at them.

Mr Heron coughed nervously. 'We also have new pupils to welcome today. Year Seven, welcome to Abergavenny High School. I hope you settle in quickly and have a happy time here. Then, in Year Eight, we have Jessica Price and David Mor . . . Morgan?'

He seemed less certain about the name for some reason. Someone stood up behind her – the boy Jessie had seen with his strange aunt outside.

'David Morgan is fine,' he said. 'Don't mind me, I won't be here long.'

His words brought a ripple of laughter. Mr Heron frowned. 'Professor Nuffield will be taking your class for geography this morning. I expect you to show the professors how well you can behave. That goes for all of you, by the way. Next, joining Year Ten . . .'

Jessie let his words wash over her. What did David Morgan mean, though, he wouldn't 'be here long'? Was he on holiday? You'd hardly go to the trouble of enrolling in a school just for a holiday. And his aunt had been weird.

The mystery of it helped her forget about being the new girl in school and the tight knot in her stomach started to unwind.

CHAPTER 9

Storm couldn't quite believe the humans had all gone out and abandoned him. Not that he cared – he was Storm of Odin who hunted lightning and ran with the thunder. Human company meant nothing to him – and anyway Jessie had said she'd be back soon. It pleased him that she was taking suitable care of his needs. And until she returned he had the whole house to himself, a silver bowl with food and one with water (not real silver, but you had to make allowances when you were dealing with humans). Also, a rug to chew on, and Jessie had left one of her sweaters over the back of a chair so he could pull it on to the floor and lie on it. What more could a young stormhound want?

But even the perfect situation can become tiresome if nothing changes, and soon Storm became restless, which was when he discovered that Jessie or her Dad had accidentally shut the door, trapping him in the room!

He pawed at the bottom of the door, growling at it to open, but it refused.

A flash of tabby fur appeared on the window sill outside.

A fine morning for hunting, Nutmeg said, sitting down to clean her whiskers. Storm barely heard her through the glass, but her smug expression was unmistakeable. *I see you're keeping your magic under control*, she said. *Well done. Most humans really don't like to think there's magic in the world.*

Most humans, Storm repeated. *You mean, some do?*

One or two, maybe, the cat said, shrugging. *I've never met one. You don't need to worry – you're safe here.*

Safe? Impertinent cat. Open the window so I may hunt with you.

I don't hunt with anyone. I am the cat who walks alone, Nutmeg said. *That comes from a book, you know.*

Do I look like I care? He didn't need a cat to assist him. Storm turned back to consider the door. It was smooth on the inside and operated by a simple, straight handle, unfortunately at human height and therefore unreachable in his current state. He jumped at it anyway, growling in frustration as his paws just caught the end of it and slid off.

You'll never open the door like that, the cat said.

I'm not listening to you.

Of course you're not. I'm only a cat. Who cares

that I've lived on this earth a mere fourteen years and seven months, while you fell out of the sky, what, last week? What could I possibly teach you? You should pay attention to how the humans do things, by the way. They've got stupid bodies, balancing along on two legs, but they're always building tools to make up for it.

He didn't need tools; he needed to be bigger, have more height. He was a stormhound, not a helpless puppy.

Watch this, cat. Storm turned and walked to the far side of the room, crouched down, tensed every muscle in his body and sprang.

His body still remembered how to fly, sort of. His paws left the ground. Storm gave a yip of triumph. He hit the door hard, kicking the handle down with his back paws.

That was when he discovered the door opened inward.

Storm bounced off the wood, turned what felt like at least five somersaults and crash-landed head-first on to the rug. He lay dazed, blinking away stars and making sure none of his limbs were broken. He didn't look at the cat: he knew she'd be laughing. As if cats never fell off things.

He picked himself up and shook himself. Tools. Looking about, he saw one of those flappy things humans used for hiding from rain. The thicker end was flimsy but the other end had a hook. Storm carried it to the door and, after several tries, he hooked it over the door handle. The cat watched from the window sill with annoying interest.

Not bad, little disciple.

I am not your disciple. And I am not little!

Whatever. Nutmeg flicked her tail at the glass. *I think the umbrella is breaking, by the way.*

What's an umbrella? The flimsy end of the rain-shelter tore, but he kept a good grip and pulled downward until the handle turned. The door creaked open. Storm dropped the broken rain-shelter and stood back, his tail wagging.

Better not let the humans find out you did that, Nutmeg advised through the window. *Humans get funny about that sort of thing.*

Much as he hated agreeing with a cat, the creature was probably right. Humans did seem to think they were the only ones who could do anything in this world. Storm returned the broken rain-shelter to its corner, then, giving himself a little shake, he padded out of the room to explore.

It was much more fun doing this without the humans hovering over him and moving him away from things, Storm discovered. Everything smelled too human, but that was easily fixed with a bit of scratching and rolling about.

There were plenty of soft places to sleep, especially upstairs. He lay down on all of them in turn to see which one he preferred, then he tried out a wooden rack of shoes by the front door. It wasn't Storm's fault that it broke when he jumped on it. *Humans ought to build better furniture. They should build better shoes too*, he thought, nosing through the pile. Not a single steel-armoured boot to try his teeth on.

After some taste-testing, he selected a furry cloth shoe that smelled of Jessie and he took it into the front room to chew on while he watched the street.

He still felt oddly empty. Guarding the house gave him something to do, but it wasn't like home. No clamour of voices and armoured feet stamping over stone floors, no sudden clash of weapons, not even the crackle and spit of a fire. All was silent.

Occasionally someone walked by outside and Storm sat up to watch them but no one challenged him. Even the shouting Valkyrie-Lady from next door walked past with barely a glance at him.

Not so brave when you're on your own, are you? Storm barked after her. She didn't look back and he lay down with a sigh.

The morning passed. Storm was dozing quietly, the shredded remains of the shoe between his paws, when he heard whistling. Opening his eyes, he saw a man striding up the short path to the house, a large bag hanging from a strap over one shoulder.

Storm leaped up. A thief! Come to fill his sack with treasure while the humans were away. Thank Odin, Storm was here to stop him.

Storm kicked the bits of shoe aside and jumped at the window. *I am Storm of Odin, temporary guardian of this dwelling. Leave your bag of treasure and flee my wrath before I smite you.*

Stupid glass. It looked flimsy, but his claws didn't even make a scratch on it. And outside, instead of running for his life, the thief paused, raised a hand in greeting and said some words Storm couldn't make out for the sound of his own barking. He was pretty sure they included the word 'puppy'.

Puppy? That's it. Prepare yourself for battle.

The glass still wouldn't break. Storm raced out of the room to the front door and flung himself against it, barking madly. His shadow filled the hallway. This was more like it. He was Storm of Odin, defender of the humans who lived here and no thief would get past him.

The metal flap in the door rattled and several objects fell through, one of them landing on Storm's head. He shook it off and stamped on it.

'Good dog,' he heard the thief say, and then rapid footsteps, fading as the intruder retreated.

Victory!

Storm bayed in triumph. But the danger was not over yet. Thieves were tricksy creatures and the things that had come through the door might contain some deadly enchantment. Storm nosed through them. Floppy rectangles made of paper that crackled satisfyingly as he chewed. He couldn't smell any magic on them, but you couldn't be too careful.

After several minutes of hard work, Storm sat back and surveyed the remains of the things littered across the hall carpet. Much better. The humans ought to do something about that flap in the door – it was most unsafe.

CHAPTER 10

'Wales is an interesting country,' Professor Nuffield said, drawing the outline of a map on the whiteboard. 'Full of myths and ancient magic.'

So far, the morning had been an odd mix. Jessie had got through the introductions in her form room. Some of the girls had wanted to know why she wasn't living in London with her mum and Jessie hadn't known quite what to say. But David had jumped in to talk about his adventures around the world with his aunt and their motorbike, and people had soon lost interest in Jessie.

Now Jessie sat sketching a portrait of Professor Nuffield in her exercise book while David sat next to her, his chin resting on his hand, his eyes half closed, nose twitching from time to time as Professor Nuffield talked. Jessie tried not to stare at the professor's moustache – it was dark blond, speckled with grey, almost the width of his plump face, and it wobbled in time with his words. His eyebrows wobbled too, but not so obviously. Jessie drew them extra bushy, adding thick lines with her pencil.

Professor Nuffield drew a final squiggly line on the board, joining up the Welsh coastline, and stood with one hand in his jacket pocket. 'Of course, any sensible person knows that magic has long since fled to the fringes of our world, along with the old gods and their stories. But some people say the Otherworld – the realm of Annwn as it's known in these parts – lies just out of mortal sight, waiting to be discovered by those who know how to see it. And, if the conditions are right, you might stumble into it without even knowing.'

A girl put up her hand. 'Sir, what does this have to do with geography?'

'Far more than you'd think,' Professor Nuffield said, sitting on the edge of his desk. 'What is geography, after all? It's the study of the land, and you can't begin to understand a land and its people until you know something of their legends. When you look at a mountain, what do you see? A pile of earth and rock, or a sleeping myth? Take Mount Skirrid for example, just a few miles from here. Why does it have that peculiar name?'

'It comes from the Welsh word *Ysgyryd*, which means "split",' David said, opening his eyes.

Professor Nuffield looked a little put out that someone knew the answer. 'Well, yes, but *why* is the mountain split? That's the important question.' He looked about, but this time no one answered.

Professor Nuffield stood and added a jagged triangle on the board – Jessie guessed it was supposed to be Mount Skirrid. 'There's a story that the devil stamped on it in a rage and broke a piece off the top,' he said. 'But I'm more inclined to blame the Wild Hunt. People in bygone ages were more superstitious than we are today. When lightning crashed around the mountains, they believed they were hearing the sound of horses and great hounds howling, and they said the Wild Hunt was riding, led by the Norse god, Odin.' He smiled. 'Or, around here, you'd say it was Arawn, King of the Otherworld. His hunting hounds are supposed to be white with red ears.'

Some of the hounds in her dream had been white with red ears, Jessie remembered, and she put down her pencil, paying attention now. She'd probably heard about them somewhere else and had forgotten. It was strange that Professor Nuffield would talk about it now, though, just after she'd dreamed about them.

She glanced at David beside her, but he'd closed his eyes again.

Professor Nuffield rested his hands on his desk, leaning forward. 'Many of these legends come from the same source, you see. The details change but the basic idea is the same. If Odin was around today, you might see a giant dog prowling in the mountains. If you do, you should stand very still. Don't even breathe. Running will trigger the hound's hunting instinct.' He stood back. 'So . . .' he asked casually, 'has anyone seen any large black or white dogs?'

A couple of people laughed.

David sighed. 'When do we get to eat?'

Jessie noticed the top of his ear was notched, as if someone had taken a piece out of it. 'How did you do that?' she asked.

He put a hand to it. 'Old injury.' He combed his hair over it with his fingers. 'My aunt said we'd learn stuff here, but this is boring.'

From what Jessie had seen of David's aunt, she felt sorry for him having someone like that for a relative. 'Where are your parents?' she whispered. 'Do they live here too?'

'No, they died.'

'Oh.' Jessie's cheeks filled up with heat. 'I'm sorry.'

'Don't be. It happened when I was a baby. I don't even remember them.'

But that would be even worse: never knowing your parents. Jessie tried to imagine it and it made her feel like she had something cold crawling inside her.

'Why did your aunt tell you to keep an eye on me?' she asked, pushing the cold feeling away.

David touched his ear again. 'She didn't. You must have misheard.'

Jessie knew she hadn't. 'She didn't like me looking at her bike.'

'She probably thought you were going to steal it or something. She gets a bit protective.' He picked up his pen and put it down again. 'Do you believe in magic?' he whispered.

Jessie stifled a laugh. 'Don't be silly.'

'You agree with Professor Nuffield, then – it's just superstition?' David looked oddly serious.

Jessie shrugged. 'I think there are a lot of things we can't explain. They can't all be superstition.'

'If you two have quite finished chatting,' Professor Nuffield said pointedly, 'maybe we could continue.'

Jessie mumbled an apology and sank lower in her seat. She wished it was lunchtime already. She wanted to go home and check on Storm. *To the house*, she corrected herself. Home was in London with Mum. This was . . . a place she had to put up with.

CHAPTER 11

After the excitement with the would-be intruder, there was very little to do in the humans' house. Storm gathered the chewed remains of the paper things into a heap and lay down by the door to sleep, one ear cocked for any noises.

Finally his patience was rewarded. Footsteps outside, the sound of a key rasping in the lock and Jessie's scent swept in. Storm jumped up.

Jessie servant! A thief brought these. Some sort of trick, but fear not! I have destroyed his evil devices. Also, your shelf for shoes broke. And some of your shoes failed to withstand my teeth. You must find yourself a better carpenter and shoemaker.

Storm watched as various emotions chased across Jessie's face. Anger at the thought of the thief, exasperation at herself for leaving the house so perilously unguarded and then laughter – thinking, no doubt, of the conversations she'd have later with the carpenter and shoemaker. He thumped his tail on the carpet. *There is no need to thank me. This is a fair bargain, the protection of a stormhound in return for your service.*

Jessie started gathering up the bits of paper and shoes.

You can do that later, Storm told her. *I require meaty chunks and a run in the garden.*

As usual, she took no notice. 'Storm, you're a naughty dog. It's a good job this was only junk mail.'

Junk mail? Was that like chain mail only not as good? And what was this nonsense about being naughty?

Jessie threw everything into a round basket. 'Why does the hall smell so funny? Have you been rolling on the carpet?'

Of course he had been. But also his shadow had spread over everything, Storm remembered. Had Jessie sensed it?

Jessie rubbed a dark patch on the wall near the door. 'I'll clean the rest later. Do you want to go out for a bit?'

Finally! He followed her through the house and waited impatiently while she opened the back door for him. Storm watched carefully, trying to work out how he could pull back the bolt and turn the key.

In the garden, the cat was nowhere to be seen, but her smell was all over the fence and the bottom of the tree.

Storm lifted his leg. *This is my tree, cat. Stay away.*

The sky was vast and grey above him, the long shape of the nearest mountain falling far short of the clouds. Storm sat and watched the sky for a while, but, apart from the drifting clouds and a few birds too far away to bother with, nothing moved.

Emptiness rose up inside him again, and he stopped the whine that formed in his chest. He must be patient. The Wild Hunt only rode at night when the skies were livid with storm, and this sky was merely sullen.

If only patience wasn't so difficult.

Storm carefully removed traces of cat smell from other parts of the garden while Jessie sat and watched. After a minute she got something square and flat and began dabbing at it with her stick again. Storm went to see what she was doing.

'I'm drawing you,' Jessie said.

Storm watched and gradually the lines took shape. A pair of ears, one of them flopping over.

I do not look like that.

Nevertheless, Storm was flattered. Jessie was a creator! He licked the paper, leaving a wet smear. The creators had a special place of honour in Odin's halls. Those who told stories or made pictures or played music. They saw the world a little differently. Storm wondered if the same thing was true of human artists. Maybe that was why Jessie had smelled the traces of magic in the hall.

Jessie pushed him away gently. 'You're dribbling on my book.'

Storm sat back and gazed up at her. *Have you ever looked up at a stormy sky and seen horses? When the Hunt returns, you can meet Odin. You will like that.*

Jessie didn't answer, and Storm left her to her drawing; she didn't appear to require help.

A door slammed in the house, followed by the sound of Jessie's Dad calling. 'Jessie? I thought I'd come home for lunch too. How was your first morning at school? What's all this stuff in the bin?'

Storm wagged his tail in greeting and went back to observing the sky.

'He's ruined the umbrella too,' Dad said. 'Storm, you're a bad boy.'

Excuse me? If it wasn't for me, your house would be full of intruders.

'He doesn't understand,' Jessie said.

She was right about that. Jessie's Dad did seem slow to grasp what was going on, even by human standards.

Jessie's Dad picked him up and carried him back into the house. 'Thank goodness we've only got to wait until Wednesday for obedience class.' He put Storm down in the middle of the floor and Jessie set the silver bowl down next to him.

Meaty chunks! Good. You are making some progress, but obedience class will help you improve faster. Hey! You've shut the door again!

CHAPTER 12

The rest of the day sped by. In school, Jessie struggled in Welsh class, but history was quite fun. The main challenge was learning everyone's names. By the end of the day, her head was spinning with them.

Meanwhile, Storm escaped from the back room again and explored the bedrooms, especially the wardrobes – he'd heard that they could lead to strange places in the Otherworld, but they all appeared quite ordinary, full of more of the humans' flimsy clothes. As night fell, Jessie sat in bed, sketching pictures of London streets, while Storm snored and twitched by her feet.

Elsewhere, on the trio of mountain peaks that surrounded Abergavenny, sheep wandered, sometimes tugging up mouthfuls of grass, but mainly just watching. Usually there wasn't much to see at night, only the trees moving in the wind and the occasional car on the roads around the mountains. Tonight, however, there was the added spectacle of three men stumbling up and down the oblong peak of the Blorenge mountain.

Professor Utterby tucked his scarf into his overcoat and shivered. Nuffield stumbled along behind, clutching a sheaf of maps while, several paces ahead, Ryston, wearing a yellow waterproof over his rabbit sweater, paused each time his divining rods twitched.

'Anything?' Utterby asked as Ryston stopped again.

Ryston stood for a moment then shook his head. 'The problem is the Welsh mountains are dappled all over with elemental magic and the rods pick up every trace. Next time, we should choose somewhere more ordinary.'

'We didn't exactly choose the spot,' Professor Utterby pointed out.

Divining rods were useful tools, and far more accurate at locating objects than Nuffield's maps. Professor Utterby had hoped that after Nuffield had given them the general location Ryston could take over the search. But his divining magic only worked with short distances. It had been pure luck that Ryston had detected a trace of Otherworld magic near the Dog Rescue Centre. Since then, they'd scoured every inch of these mountains and found nothing.

Of course, the problem might be Ryston himself. He was the youngest and the least experienced of them all. He'd only become a full professor this year, and then only because he'd nagged Professor Utterby into it. In centuries gone by, there'd have been twenty different exams, practical tests and you'd have to complete your own area of special research before you could even become a Doctor of Magic, let alone a Professor.

'Maybe we should split up,' Nuffield suggested.

Professor Utterby snorted. 'And if you find the stormhound on your own, how exactly will you capture it? Or are you hoping we'll deduce the creature's location from your remains?'

Ryston sat down, breathing hard. 'You know the tears of a stormhound are supposed to cure all injuries? Does that include asthma?'

'Probably,' Professor Utterby said distractedly. 'We'll give it a try and see, if you like.' He heard a sound behind him and swung round with a yelp of alarm, half expecting to see a giant hound creeping up on him, but it was only a sheep. 'Yes, very clever,' Utterby said, flapping his hands at it.

How could a giant hound have disappeared so thoroughly?

As the professors made their way down the Blorenge, a pair of white hares bounded up to an orange-and-black motorbike that stood beside a hedge at the foot of the Sugar Loaf mountain on the other side of town. The air shimmered and the two hares became two people.

David pulled grass out of his hair. 'I've missed that. We should do it more often.'

His aunt frowned. 'I raised you to be a boy, not a wild animal, Morfran. Please act like it. We use magic when necessary, not for our own amusement.'

David fought the urge to scratch himself with his back leg. He liked being a boy: it was useful to be able to stand up straight, and of course thumbs were really good. But as a boy, he couldn't run nearly as fast, and his hearing and sense of smell weren't as sensitive. Anyway, if Ceridwen wanted him to be a boy, why did she keep calling him by the name she'd given him when she'd found him as a hare all those years ago?

'Why can't you just go and zap the professors?' he asked. 'You said they're black magicians, right? So whatever they're doing must be something to do with black magic.'

Ceridwen gave him a look halfway between amusement and irritation. 'I do not "zap" people. You don't know the professors like I do. They've always been dabblers in dark magic. An occasional nuisance rather than a serious threat. When they went quiet two years ago, I thought they'd finally given up. And now they're back.'

Back, and searching the mountains. David pulled another piece of grass from his hair and nibbled it. 'The question is, then, what were they doing for those two years?'

'Exactly,' his aunt said, nodding. 'They've discovered something, that much is clear. It must be something big to draw them all here – some powerful artefact that's lain here for centuries. It may even be a bigger danger than the professors themselves.'

A powerful artefact sounded like fun, though David didn't say so. He knew what Auntie Ceridwen would think of that, and he could imagine the lecture she'd give him on the safe and proper disposal of magical objects. He followed her back to the bike and picked up his helmet in silence.

'You'll just have to get closer to the professors tomorrow,' Ceridwen said. 'That girl too. I checked the camouflage spells on the bike and they're all working. She should not have seen me. Talk to her again.'

'And say what?' David asked. 'I don't think she likes me.'

'Then try harder. Be friendly. Pretend you're an ordinary boy who's just started school. We need answers.'

Another day in school. David sighed. It ought to be exciting, protecting the world from dark magic. Why did he always have to do the boring jobs?

CHAPTER 13

The second day at school didn't feel quite so strange as the first. Jessie knew the layout of the building now, so it was easier to find her way around. She was starting to remember names too. Charlotte and Megan on the desk next to her, and Prisha who'd said hello a few times. She'd tell Dad about it later, and make it sound like she was happily making new friends. He'd like that. Mum too – she'd phoned this morning while Jessie was getting ready for school and the first thing she'd asked was whether Jessie was making friends. As if you could replace all your old friends in a single day.

'Jessica Price, are you paying attention?' the teacher asked.

Jessie jumped and sat upright. 'Sorry.' She had no idea what he'd just asked.

'He wants to know when Shakespeare wrote *Macbeth,*' David said, beside her. 'The answer is 1606.'

The teacher frowned. 'I didn't ask you, David.'

David glowered. 'What's his problem?' he

whispered to Jessie. 'He wanted to know the answer so I told him. I was trying to help.'

Jessie smiled despite her annoyance. 'You're supposed to let other people answer.'

'But that would take twice as long. ' He folded his arms and sighed. 'This place is stupid.'

Jessie ignored him until the bell for break rang and everyone scrambled up. She started to follow people outside but felt a tug on her sleeve.

'Wait,' David said.

Jessie paused in surprise. 'What?'

'Nothing.' He scooped his bag up and stood, shifting from one foot to the other. 'What exactly are we supposed to do at breaktime? It was a bit confusing yesterday with everyone rushing about.'

'We're not supposed to do anything. That's why it's called a break.' Jessie grinned. 'You weren't joking when you said you hadn't been to school before, were you?'

He shrugged uncomfortably. 'Auntie Ceridwen normally teaches me herself. She says it's more efficient.'

Jessie imagined the stern-faced woman standing at the front of a class consisting only of David. It didn't sound much fun to her. 'What does your aunt do for a living?' she asked. 'My dad's an accountant. He's just started work with the council.' She put out a hand to stop him. 'You're going the wrong way. We're supposed to go outside for break – it's in the school rules.'

David flicked his hair back. 'I have enough rules from my aunt. Anyway, what's Mr Heron going to do? I'm not going to be here long.'

He said it defiantly and scowled, but it was the sort of way Ben talked when he was pretending everything was all right.

'What kind of job means you have to move about all the time?' she asked. 'Can't your aunt get something in one place and stay there?' *Whatever she does, seeing as you still haven't told me.*

David gave a short laugh. 'She'd go mad stuck in one place. We arrive somewhere, stay just as long as we need to, then Auntie Ceridwen will be off somewhere else, and I go with her. I guess it might be nice having somewhere to call home, but it's a waste of time wishing for something you can't have.'

Like how she'd longed for a dog, or the way she wished she were back in London. Jessie sighed. Dad had hoped Storm would make her feel at home here, but it hadn't worked. She loved Storm, but in some way it had made things worse because now half of her wanted to stay with Storm forever, and the other half wanted to go back home, to London, with Mum and all her friends.

Still, maybe she could start making friends here.

'We've got IT next,' she said. 'Do you want to sit together?'

Then she stopped because Professor Utterby came out of a classroom, wiping his hands on his jacket. A little trail of smoke followed him. He paused when he saw Jessie and David, his eyebrows jumping.

'Good morning, Professor Utterby,' Jessie said. 'Did you know your jacket is on fire?'

'Is it?' He patted at it until the smoke disappeared. 'You want to go outside to play.'

It wasn't a question, or even a statement. It was a command. And, Jessie found, she really did want to go outside. For a moment or two, the feeling was overwhelming. She turned round and was halfway to the school doors before she knew what was happening. She paused and looked back. Professor Utterby had gone, and so had David.

David was already in the computer lab when Jessie arrived, sitting at a table by the window and staring out. Following his gaze, Jessie saw Professor Ryston walking to and fro in the car park, holding something that glinted – those pieces of metal Jessie had seen in his pocket before.

'What's he doing?' she asked.

'No idea.' David kept watching, his gaze following Professor Ryston's path up and down.

Jessie sighed and turned on the computer. They

were supposed to be designing a poster for the school's Autumn Fayre, something she should have loved doing, but she couldn't concentrate. She glanced around to make sure no one was watching her, then she opened the web browser and typed in 'Bangor University'.

The site came up straight away. Jessie started searching through the various pages, looking for any mention of the professors. They'd said they were on secondment from Bangor.

But there was nothing. No photos, nothing on the list of lecturers, no mention of any secondment scheme. The website might be out of date, of course, but somehow Jessie didn't think so. Yet if the professors weren't from Bangor, where *were* they from? She nudged David.

'What?' he asked.

'I'm trying to look up the professors online and I can't find a thing about them. Don't you think that's odd?'

'Not really. Not everyone is online.' He went back to staring out of the window.

He was wrong: there ought to be something. Jessie frowned at the screen. Professor Nuffield had been talking about the Wild Hunt and Mount Skirrid in geography class yesterday. Maybe he was an expert on that. Jessie opened another web browser and looked up 'Skirrid Mountain'. There were various legends about the mountain, but none of them mentioned the Wild Hunt or the Hounds of Annwn. Professor Nuffield wasn't such an expert, after all. She found some pictures of the Wild Hunt, though – riders on horseback surrounded by hunting hounds, racing through the sky.

Jessie paused and glanced sideways at David. He was still watching Professor Ryston through the window.

'Why are you so interested in the professors?' she asked. 'You ran off right after Professor Utterby spoke to us earlier too. Were you hiding from him?'

David jerked his gaze from the window. 'Forget about the professors, all right?'

He moved into the next seat away from her and turned on the computer, although he still kept looking out of the window. At one point, Professor Ryston looked up and David shrank back as if he didn't want to be seen.

Jessie tried to ignore both of them but she couldn't. Something just felt wrong and she couldn't explain why. David's aunt was called Ceridwen, wasn't she? Jessie doubted anything would come up, but she typed in the name anyway.

The very first entry read:

Ceridwen is an enchantress from Welsh legend.
According to the Tale of Taliesin, she had a son

called Morfran who was hideously ugly.

Ceridwen, wanting to give her son great wisdom, brewed a potion. It took her a year and the mixture had to be stirred constantly. She employed a young boy to do it, but at the end of the year, while he was stirring, three drops of potion splashed on to his hand and he licked them off. Immediately he gained all the wisdom meant for Morfran.

'Now what are you looking at?' David asked, looking over.

Jessie closed the web browser quickly. 'Nothing.'

She went back to designing a poster. So David's aunt was named after a Welsh enchantress. And his surname, Morgan, was only a couple of letters away from Morfran. Was that the name Mr Heron had been trying to read when he'd said David Morgan? But what did that have to do with the professors?

Nothing, she told herself. She was inventing mysteries to pass the time.

But then, right at the end of the day when everyone was leaving, Jessie saw David doubling back through the school doors. She paused.

What's he doing?

He'd probably forgotten something. She should mind her own business. If he wanted to get into trouble, it was up to him.

On the other hand, she didn't have to hurry home. Ben had football practice, Dad would still be at work and Storm wouldn't mind waiting a few minutes. Anyway, David shouldn't keep disappearing and behaving so mysteriously if he didn't want to be followed.

Jessie ran back into the school. She saw David almost at once, walking down a corridor. She hid round the corner and watched. *This was silly. There were any number of reasons why he'd go back into school.*

David stopped outside a classroom, put his hand to the closed door and then he leaned in and sniffed it.

All right – maybe there weren't many reasons for that. Jessie shifted her weight from foot to foot, wondering whether to ask what he was doing, but before she could decide what to do the door opened.

David jumped back, rubbing his nose as Professor Ryston emerged.

'What are you doing, boy?' he asked. 'What's your name?' He looked closer. 'Have I seen you before?'

'No, I don't think so,' David said, backing away.

Jessie's heart thumped. David really looked scared of the professor.

'He was waiting for me,' Jessie said, stepping out of hiding. 'We're going back to my house for tea. I was, um, using the toilet.' She ran and grabbed David's arm. 'Come on,' she said, pulling him away. 'Dad's waiting outside. And I can see Mr Heron.'

She couldn't see Mr Heron at all – she just hoped Professor Ryston would let them go if he thought the head was coming. She was right. He stepped back away from them.

'I'll be keeping an eye on you,' he said.

That was almost what David's aunt had said yesterday morning but somehow Professor Ryston made it sound a lot more threatening. Jessie nodded and fled, towing David behind her. They didn't stop until they were outside the school.

'What were you doing?' Jessie asked.

'Nothing.' David pulled his arm free. 'Why are you so nosy?'

'Because you won't tell me what's going on. You know who the professors are, don't you? You and your aunt.'

David laughed. 'What makes you think that?'

'The fact you were just spying on Professor Ryston, for a start.' She folded her arms and stared at him. 'Did you know your aunt's named after a Welsh sorcerer?'

His cheeks turned pink. 'An enchantress, actually, but yes. She's proud of it. Why?'

'No reason. It's just interesting. You know, with Professor Nuffield being interested in legends, and you being interested in the professors. Everything feels out of place here and I don't like it.'

David gave a weak smile and brushed a hand across his hair. 'Now you sound like Auntie Ceridwen. *Everything has its proper place and that's where it should stay.*'

'The world doesn't work like that, though, does it?' Jessie said. 'My proper place is in London. Where's yours?'

She didn't think anyone had ever asked David that before. He blinked at her in confusion, then looked down at his feet. It was moment before he answered.

'I haven't got one.'

He sounded forlorn, all of a sudden: lost – the way Storm had looked in the shelter.

'Do you really have to go straight home?' Jessie asked. 'You can come for tea if you like. You can tell your aunt you were keeping an eye on me.'

'She didn't say that,' David said, but then he flashed her a grin. 'All right, she did say it. She thought you looked interesting, that's all. She didn't mean anything bad by it. I'm a vegetarian – is that OK?'

Jessie had expected him to say no, and she grinned in return. 'So's Ben. Come on, you can meet Storm.'

CHAPTER 14

Storm was worried. For a start, there'd been no sign of the Wild Hunt in the two weeks since he'd fallen and they should surely have come looking for him by now. More than that, though, he was beginning to suspect a different kind of trouble was brewing. Everything about the human world was so strange he couldn't tell what was considered normal here, but several times today he'd found himself jerking out of sleep, his coat prickling in alarm. And, when Jessie had let him into the garden at midday, he'd caught the scent of magic coming off the mountain. That surely wasn't normal in the human world.

It took a little longer to open the back-room door, but Storm managed it, wandering into the front room and jumping on to the top of the seat so he could watch the street outside. Jessie had returned by this time, yesterday. Was she going to come back at a different time every day just to vex him?

Then he saw her coming along the road. Storm jumped up at the window, his tail wagging. He was so pleased to see her he didn't notice an important fact: she wasn't alone. It wasn't until she opened the door and called his name that he caught the invader's scent, and he stopped so fast his claws got stuck in the carpet. Whatever that creature was, he was not a boy. He might look human, with his two arms and legs and hairless skin, but his smell made Storm think of fur and blood, and there was something else too – a faint but unmissable spark of magic.

Storm flattened himself to the floor, his whole body quivering.

'Storm, what are you doing? Stop it!' Jessie scooped him up and carried him into the kitchen. The Not-Boy kept his distance. Good. He had no business walking about on two legs, looking like a boy. He was picking up Jessie's book of pictures now, turning the pages, and she didn't even seem to mind.

'These are good,' the Not-Boy said. 'I like the one of Storm.'

'Thanks. I haven't finished it yet.' Jessie put Storm down and took his lead off its hook. 'I usually take him for a walk in the afternoon. Do you mind? I can let him out in the garden for a while otherwise.'

Not the garden! He needed to stay here and protect Jessie from this creature.

The Not-Boy peered around Jessie at him. Storm crouched lower. *Hide your magic*, the cat had said. He kept his shadow drawn in beneath him and gazed at the Not-Boy with innocent eyes.

The Not-Boy frowned and shook his head. 'We can go for a walk if you like. As long as I don't have to walk next to him. I mean, he's cute, but I was bitten by a dog once.' He rubbed the top of his ear.

I'll bite the other ear off for you if you call me cute again. What did Jessie think she was doing? Did humans have no sense, inviting strange creatures into their homes? Storm retreated under a chair, staring at the Not-Boy between the legs.

Jessie pulled him out and clipped the lead to his collar. 'So, what were you doing spying on Professor Ryston?' she asked.

The Not-Boy continued flipping through the pages of Jessie's book. 'I wasn't spying on him – not specifically. Why were you spying on me?'

'I wasn't,' Jessie said. 'Not specifically.'

The Not-Boy grinned and turned to the last page of the book. 'What are all these scribbles?'

'Nothing.' She was tense suddenly, though Storm didn't know why. He ran to the door, tugging on his leash, and she seemed relieved to follow.

Outside, clouds drifted over the sun, so that the afternoon was bright one moment and the next everything looked grey.

'I wish the weather would make up its mind what it wants to be,' Jessie said. 'I have a theory. Your Auntie Ceridwen is a reporter for the TV, and the professors are celebrities in disguise.'

Ceridwen? Professors? TV? Why did humans talk in riddles?

'Not even close,' the Not-Boy said. 'Why did your dad decide to come here? Have you ever lived in Wales before?'

'I don't think he decided – it's just where he found a job.' Jessie twisted Storm's lead round her hand. 'We came to Wales on holiday once, but that was further north. I almost got struck by lightning.'

She hadn't said anything about lightning before. Storm paused and sniffed at her leg. Jessie reached down to scratch his head. 'I was only four, so I don't remember it. We were in a cottage near Snowdon. Dad says there was this huge flash of lighting and that's when he realized the door was open and I was missing. He ran outside and found me under the remains of a tree, half a field away. Dad will tell you all about it if you ask him. I think he's disappointed it didn't give me superpowers.'

She walked on, but the Not-Boy grew quite still for a moment. 'Maybe it did,' he said.

Jessie laughed. 'Yes, I'm a superhero. And your aunt's a detective, you're her sidekick and the professors are bank robbers. They've hidden a big stash of stolen money, but they've forgotten where it is – that's what Professor Ryston was looking for.'

The Not-Boy snorted. 'That's even worse than your

celebrity idea. Why would bank robbers come to a tiny place like this?'

A tiny place? Storm barked. *Haven't you seen the mountains, haven't you looked at the vast, empty sky?* He walked on, puzzling. Why would anyone want to rob a bank, anyway? He'd seen river banks and they were generally made of mud. He tugged on his lead. *Hey, let's go to the river now. I like it there.*

Jessie tugged him back in the opposite direction. Storm heaved a sigh. He needed a better way of making these humans understand him. They weren't doing a very good job of it at the moment.

'This is nice,' the Not-Boy said after a while. 'I don't usually get the chance to hang about town. Not with other people.'

He sounded lonely, even for a boy who wasn't human. How many other people felt lost in this world, with nowhere to belong?

'Don't you ever make friends?' Jessie asked.

The Not-Boy stuffed his hands in his pockets. 'I used to. But as soon as I get to know people it's time to leave. This is the first place I've even been to school.'

Storm didn't know whether that was normal or not, but he guessed it wasn't.

'What *does* your aunt do?' Jessie asked. 'It must be something important for you to live like that.'

'It is – *very* important. She doesn't like me talking about it.'

Keep asking questions, Storm urged Jessie silently. *He's getting nervous. There's something he doesn't want to tell you. Lots of things, probably.*

He tugged her on and tried to get between her and the Not-Boy, just in case he needed to defend her, but then he caught a scent that made him stop.

Magic, stronger than anything he'd smelled yet, even from the Not-Boy. It completely eclipsed Jessie's tiny lightning spark. Storm charged forward, forgetting about the leash until it snapped tight. He skidded to a stop as a tall woman came round the corner.

She was human, but not like any human Storm had met yet. She smelled like she'd been carved out of the mountains and had lived in this world for a very long time.

The Not-Boy edged backwards. 'Auntie Ceridwen, this is Jessie.'

'You're that girl,' the woman said, staring.

One step closer and Storm would spring at her. Except that he couldn't because of the annoying leash. And he'd only reach her knees at best. Her gaze made Storm painfully aware of his smallness, how weak he was in this body. He lay down and rested his head on his paws.

'I asked David to stay for tea,' Jessie said. 'Is that all right?'

The woman kept staring. 'No, I think it isn't all

right. We're not here to socialize – *David.*'

The Not-Boy flinched, but Jessie's lightning scent sparked, growing sharp and angry.

'It's not like I asked him to rob a bank with me,' Jessie said. 'There's no need to be mean.'

'Leave it,' the Not-Boy whispered.

For the first time, Storm agreed with him.

Jessie shook her head. 'No. You said yourself you never get the chance to make friends. It's not fair of your aunt to stop you.' Her voice rose, reminding Storm of how she'd shouted at the Valkyrie-Lady from next door.

The aunt took another step forward. Storm growled. She flicked a glance at him and he shrank back, struggling to keep his shadow under control.

'Jessie only started school yesterday,' the Not-Boy said, stepping in front of her. 'She doesn't know anything.'

'Then you don't need to waste any more time here,' the aunt said. 'Come along.'

She turned away, clearly expecting the Not-Boy to follow, but he didn't move.

'No,' he said. 'Jessie invited me for tea. You know, like friends do. I'm staying.'

The aunt stood for a second as if turned to stone. Storm had never seen a human looking so surprised before. He wondered what the aunt would say, or whether she'd drag the Not-Boy away. Instead, she

99

shook her head slowly and then she sighed.

'You're growing up,' she said, dropping her gaze to the pavement. She seemed lost for a moment, but when she looked at the Not-Boy again, there was a hint of pride in her eyes. 'All right,' she said, 'we'll talk about this later. Don't stay out too long.'

Storm watched her walk away, embarrassed at how relieved he felt. The Not-Boy grinned. 'Don't mind her. She worries about me, that's all.' But Storm could see he was shaking.

'You don't have to stay for tea,' Jessie told him.

'No, I want to. I'm tired of her telling me what to do all the time.' He blew out a breath of air. 'Look, you're right about the professors, sort of. They're not real professors – not from Bangor University, anyway.'

'Then your aunt *is* investigating them,' Jessie said. She jiggled on her toes. If she had a tail, she'd be wagging it. 'I knew it! But why did you tell her I don't know anything? Was she worried I'd guess the truth?'

The Not-Boy hunched his shoulders. 'Something like that. Please, do me a favour and stop asking questions. You said before there are things in the world that can't be explained. Just pretend this is one of them. And stay away from the professors.'

'Why?' Jessie asked. 'Are they evil criminal masterminds?'

The Not-Boy walked on down the road. 'I'm not answering any more questions.'

'I'm right, aren't I?' Jessie persisted, following him. 'You're helping her spy on them. If you told me about it, I could help you.' The Not-Boy didn't answer, and she sighed. 'All right, keep your secrets. As long as you're not in any trouble.'

She sounded fierce, as if she were ready to fight the Not-Boy's aunt for him – which would be a very bad idea. Jessie had no idea about magic, she was just trying to help a friend, it seemed.

Storm whined softly. Who were these mysterious professors and what did the Not-Boy and his aunt want with them?

'Tired?' Jessie asked, picking Storm up. He wriggled deeper into her jacket, his ridiculous puppy ears flopping over his eyes.

Don't worry. I'll protect you, he promised. *From Not-Boys and aunts and professors too*. Even though he was tiny, even though she was the one who was carrying him when it should be the other way round, he was still a stormhound inside and, until the Hunt returned, this was his territory. He would defend it. Somehow.

CHAPTER 15

Professor Utterby sat at a desk in the school staffroom they'd acquired from Mr Heron. The headmaster had been most obliging once Professor Utterby had thrown the right combination of powders in his face and explained that they needed their own private workspace. A few days ago, this had been a classroom. Now, the tables and chairs had gone, replaced by three large armchairs, a coffee table in the middle of the room, a TV and a bookshelf holding a collection of books, most of which you wouldn't find in any school.

Professor Utterby glanced irritably at Nuffield, who was eating cheese-and-onion crisps from a giant-sized bag. 'Do you have to crunch like that?' he asked. 'I have a chemistry class in half an hour and I am trying to prepare.'

Nuffield shoved another handful of crisps into his mouth. A few pieces stuck to his moustache and wobbled there. The coffee table in front of him was covered in maps, and most of them were covered in red lines.

'Where's Ryston?' he asked. 'I want to ask him something.'

'Year Ten are hard work,' Ryston said, opening the door, coming in and dropping into a chair. 'They kept asking me about Renaissance painters, like I actually know anything about art. Are you sure you cast the confusion spells on the school properly, Utterby?'

'Of course I'm sure,' Utterby said. 'What's the point of being a Professor of Forbidden Magic if you can't cast spells properly?'

'Never mind Year Ten,' Nuffield said. 'Come and look at this.' He rummaged through the maps on the coffee table. Professor Utterby walked across to look.

'I fail to see how you can find the stormhound by drawing on maps,' he said, sneering.

Professor Nuffield emptied the last of the crisps into his mouth. 'That's where you're wrong. I've been checking the weather. I believe we can expect a storm, roughly here.' He pointed to a circle he'd drawn round the top of Mount Skirrid. 'Am I right?'

Ryston picked up his divining rods and held them over the map. Professor Utterby watched with interest as they began to swing in circles then stopped abruptly.

'Friday,' Ryston said.

Professor Utterby frowned. 'Are you sure?'

'Of course I'm sure. This Friday, the seventh of September, starting in the early afternoon and continuing into the evening. Four o'clock looks like the peak time.' His divining rods dipped together, swinging low to touch the map at the same place. 'If we miss that one, the next storm isn't for a month, at least.'

He put down the rods and wrote *7 September, 4 p.m.* on the top of the map.

So they had until Friday to find the stormhound, or they'd have to wait another month for conditions to only be half as good. A storm, especially a storm on a mountaintop, meant there'd be lots of energy flowing about. The stormhound's power would be at its peak. More dangerous to kill it then, yes, but the reward would be far greater.

'So we have the time and the place,' Utterby said. 'All we need is the animal.' They could do it, he thought, ignoring the fact that, so far, they'd only succeeded in finding places where the stormhound *wasn't* hiding. At least they were ruling things out. The stormhound wasn't hiding in the mountains, so maybe it was hiding in plain sight, here in the town.

The notion was so ludicrous he could have laughed. What had Nuffield said? It could be a small stormhound, only the size of a Great Dane.

Ludicrous, but worth a try. Professor Utterby returned to his desk and started gathering up half-filled glass jars of various liquids and powders. 'I have a chemistry class to teach. After that, we will take the rest of the day off school. Start looking for parks, dog-walking groups, anywhere where dogs may assemble.'

CHAPTER 16

'Chemistry,' Professor Utterby said, 'is the basis of existence.'

Jessie sat at the back of the science lab, not really paying attention. Her head felt like it was full of bricks this morning. She'd slept badly last night, dreaming of storm clouds and giant dogs again, and she'd filled another two pages of her sketchbook in her sleep. Instead of random lines, she'd drawn a tree standing in a field, slashes of rain cutting across the page.

Her phone buzzed in her bag. She sneaked a look – a message from Mum: *Sorry I didn't answer this morning. In a meeting. I'll call tonight. Love you xxx.*

At the front of the class, Professor Utterby began connecting up a Bunsen burner and clearing space around it. Jessie put her phone away and nudged David.

'I know what it is. The professors aren't criminals. They're witnesses to a crime and they're in hiding. Your aunt is protecting them to make sure the real criminals don't find them.'

David pretended to be writing. Jessie grabbed his pen. 'Don't ignore me.'

'Keep your voice down,' David muttered.

'Or what? Professor Utterby will hear us?'

David took his pen back. 'Everyone will hear you if you carry on like that. No, they're not witnesses in hiding. Be quiet.'

Professor Utterby took a marker pen out of his pocket. 'Once people talked about the four elements,' he said. 'Air, earth, water and fire. Now we know there are many more – one hundred and three at the last count. Everything is made of chemical elements. This table, your books, your pens and pencils – in fact, all of *you* – are made of chemicals. Once you can identify those chemicals you can start to control them, and that means you can control anything.'

He drew a star around the burner in five confident strokes on the desk.

'What's that for?' a dark-haired girl asked. Prisha, Jessie remembered.

Professor Utterby snapped the cap back on the pen. 'A precaution. If you go to university, you'll learn a lot of advanced science like this.'

It didn't look like science. Jessie sat forward, watching as Professor Utterby lit the burner and laid out jars, packets and bottles in a careful semi-circle around it.

'We'll begin with the common elements,' he said,

opening a packet. He had everyone's attention now. 'Watch closely, please. This is what happens when you add sea salt to flame.' He looked up, his gaze sweeping the class. 'Needless to say, do not try any of these experiments at home. Higher elemental chemistry is very dangerous and has unpredictable results. Especially when you use fire.'

He sprinkled a few white crystals over the burner. The flame turned yellow for a few seconds, fizzled and settled.

Was that supposed to happen?

A grumble of disappointment ran around the classroom.

'Boring,' Professor Utterby announced. 'Sea and flame are not natural friends. They're not exactly enemies, but they prefer to ignore each other if they can get away with it. Put them together and they'll nod to each other as they pass, but that's all the reaction you'll see.' He opened a second packet. 'Now, this is also common salt, but this time it is mountain salt, not sea salt. Water is weak, always sloshing about in tides and using up its energy, but mountains have stood since this country first took shape. Soaking up the energy of the earth – the changing seasons, the passing storms. And, as everyone knows, mountains love fire. Their shape, leaping into the sky, mimics the leap of flame. And have you noticed how lightning always aims for high places? Lightning is fire contained, and fire always seeks out the places of power.'

Prisha raised her hand. 'Sir, are you sure this is on the chemistry syllabus?'

Professor Utterby paused, eyebrows in mid-raise. 'As William Shakespeare said, there are more things in heaven and earth than you can dream about. You'd do well to remember that and maintain an open mind. Open minds let the most information in.'

He poured a few crystals of mountain salt into his palm and tilted his hand for the class to see. The grains looked exactly the same as the sea salt.

'Observe,' Professor Utterby said. He adjusted the burner and cast the salt into the flame.

Bang!

The explosion shot flame up to the ceiling. All the windows rattled. Jessie ducked and several people shouted in alarm.

'That is the power of the mountains,' Professor Utterby said with a satisfied smile.

Jessie rubbed her eyes, blinking away purple afterimages of the burner.

Professor Utterby picked up a jar that appeared to be empty. 'Now let us see what happens when we mix fire with invisible nitrate.'

This was definitely not on any chemistry syllabus.

The class piled out of the lab to break, chattering noisily.

'Did you see when he put potassium into water?' Prisha said.

Jessie paused. 'He didn't use potassium. Or water. He threw salt into a flame and it nearly set fire to the classroom.'

Prisha blinked at her. 'It was potassium. I wrote it down.' She flicked through her exercise book, frowning at the blank pages. 'I must have forgotten. Never mind.'

She wandered on.

Jessie turned to see David staring at her. 'What?' she asked.

'Nothing.' But he kept staring at her. 'You remember what happened in class, don't you?'

'Of course I remember,' Jessie said. 'We've only just come out.'

She knew what he meant, though. Everyone else seemed to think it was an ordinary chemistry lesson – she and David were the only ones to remember it properly.

'How did Professor Utterby do that?' she asked. She remembered the other day when he'd ordered her to go outside and she'd started to obey without thinking. 'Is it hypnosis or something?'

'You wouldn't believe me if I told you,' David said.

'I might do. I believe lots of things.'

'No you don't. The bigger question is, why didn't it work on you?'

'Given that I don't know what any of this is about, I have no idea. How about magic? The professors are evil magicians and your aunt is the magic police come to arrest them.'

David gave her an odd look. Jessie laughed. 'Come on, tell me the truth. Are you being deliberately weird just to annoy me?'

'I'm never deliberately weird – it just happens.' He gave a half-smile, then pushed his hands in his pockets and frowned. 'You said you wanted to help – did you mean it?'

Jessie returned his smile. 'Yes, of course. What do you need?'

David pulled her further down the corridor, glancing about. 'You were right, partly,' he said quietly. 'My aunt *is* investigating the professors. I can't tell you why, but I need to get into their staffroom after school and look around. If you come with me, I think we might get away with it.'

Yes, because two people breaking in is far less noticeable than one. Dad would kill her if he found out. On the other hand, she had offered to help, and she had to admit this was more exciting than her school in London had ever been. She slung her bag firmly over her shoulder. After that non-chemistry class, she'd like to know what the professors' room looked like.

'All right,' she said. 'When do you want to do it?'

CHAPTER 17

'Are you sure you saw the professors leave?' Jessie whispered. Her palms felt clammy. Standing outside the professors' staffroom after everyone else had gone home for the day, this was feeling more and more like a giant-sized mistake.

'Yes, I'm sure,' David said. 'Don't worry. If anyone *is* there, we'll say we have a question about class.'

She had lots of questions, Jessie thought, but she wasn't sure it would be safe to ask them. She tried the door and found it locked.

'Let me try,' David said. He turned the handle, then bent to blow into the keyhole. A moment later, the door opened. 'Must have been a bit stiff,' he said, straightening up.

'Yes,' Jessie agreed, not quite believing him. If his aunt was an investigator, maybe he had special lock-picking skills or something. She stepped into the room, letting her breath out slowly when she saw it was empty. 'What exactly are we looking for?' she asked.

'Anything that doesn't belong in a staffroom.'

That wasn't much help – nothing seemed to belong here. Jessie picked a crisp packet up off the floor and dropped it into the bin. *Don't drop litter* was one of the first school rules. Mr Heron would have a fit if he saw the state of this room.

David started opening books, frowning as he flipped through the pages. Most of the titles were in foreign languages, but there was a book of Welsh legends, and another one on mythical creatures.

'That's not important,' David said as Jessie reached for it. He put back the book he was reading and turned to the desk, poking open a box and jumping back as if the contents might be dangerous. Jessie looked, and saw marker pens and candles, and a set of jars full of coloured powders. More of Professor Utterby's chemistry equipment, she guessed. She picked up two of the maps from the coffee table and laid them side by side. Her breath came too fast and the skin on her back itched every time she took her attention off the door. She pulled another map from under the pile and paused as she recognized the name 'Mount Skirrid'. Someone had circled the central contour in red ink, and written a date: *7 September, 4 p.m.*

David snatched the map away, making her jump. 'Don't touch those. You might leave fingerprints.'

'Fingerprints? On paper?'

'You never know.' David stared at the map,

frowning, and ran his finger over the red circle of ink that surrounded Mount Skirrid. He wasn't that worried about fingerprints, then.

'They're going to do something, aren't they?' she asked. 'And this is the place and the time. But what are they planning?'

'I have no idea.' David held up a hand as she opened her mouth to argue. 'Really, I don't. I need to tell my aunt about this. We should get out of here before someone sees us.'

They slipped back out and David shut the door. Jessie was trembling. She couldn't believe they'd got away with it. She had to swallow a fit of giggles as they raced down the corridor to the main doors. Mr Heron came out of the school office.

'The bell rang fifteen minutes ago,' he said. 'What are you still doing here?'

'Sorry,' Jessie gasped. 'We got lost.'

They ran outside. Jessie paused by the gates, waiting for the stitch in her side to go away. 'What do you want to do now? I'm taking Storm to obedience class later but you can come home with me for a bit if you like.'

David shook his head. 'I'd better go back and tell my aunt what I found. Then I might hang around town a bit, see if the professors do anything else. See you tomorrow? And please don't say anything about this to anyone.'

'Of course not,' Jessie said.

She set off home, and she was halfway there when she suddenly stopped.

Home, she'd said. She called the house 'home', and it had slipped out so naturally she hadn't even noticed. She ought to be happy, she supposed, but instead it felt like something cold had settled inside her. She already had a home, in London with Mum. She didn't want another one.

CHAPTER 18

It was the evening of Wednesday – Woden's Day – which felt like a good day to begin training the humans in obedience. Yet, so far, the obedience class had proved a sorry disappointment.

Six other dogs stood around the edges of a cold hall: a Great Dane as tall as a small pony, a yellow Labrador who smelled of wet pavements and four dogs of various mixed breeds, all smelling of the rain that still pattered against the windows. The hall smelled of even more dogs, their scents fading in and out of one another, some quite recent, others at least a week old.

The Great Dane trod on Storm's paw. *Watch it, little one.*

Little one? Identify yourself, Storm snapped.

The Great Dane looked down at him, wagging his tail in puzzlement. *I am Viking. This is my human, Henry.*

Storm looked up at the skinny human who held the end of Viking's leash. He was displaying a woeful lack of obedience, talking to the lady next to him and ignoring his canine master altogether.

Storm was surprised at the differences between humans. When you ran across the sky, there was very little time for looking down, and Storm had always assumed humans were more or less the same. He was finding out how wrong he'd been about that. There were tall humans and short ones, fat and thin. They all had different smells, which changed subtly, depending on the time of day. They all had names as well, and it appeared that the more important they were in the human world, the more names they had. Jessie's father, for example, was called Dad and Mr Price and Stephen, depending on who was talking to him. Jessie was just Jessie, which seemed strange because she was the most important of all.

Storm turned back to Viking. *What exactly do we do here?*

The Great Dane shrugged, making dark ripples move down his coat. *It's our quiz night. The humans have crunchy treats and we have to work out how to get them. But the humans keep changing the rules to make it harder.*

Wait a minute. Storm bristled. *The humans set the rules?*

You don't have to follow them, one of the other dogs chimed in. *It depends how much you like crunchy treats.*

'Come away, Viking,' Henry muttered, tugging the dog away a few steps. Jessie picked Storm up and hugged him. He sniffed at her face. It was strange how he felt more puppyish when she was with him. The door opened and Storm stiffened in Jessie's arms, then began to scrabble at her as the Fuzzy-Lady from the dog prison came in.

'I'm sorry I'm late,' she said. 'The weather is awful today.'

You! Foul lady, you will not take me back to the place of comfortable confinement.

'Sorry,' Jessie said, putting Storm back on the floor. He wasn't sure whether she was addressing him or foul Fuzzy-Lady. No matter. He'd wasted enough time here. *Follow me,* he commanded, tugging on the annoying leash Jessie had attached to his collar. *Let us return to your dwelling.*

Jessie tugged back. 'Come here, Storm.'

You're not very good at this obedience thing, are you?

Fuzzy-Lady smiled and reached out to take the end of the leash from Jessie. 'Don't worry. We all have to start at the beginning. How are you getting on together?'

We are getting on fine. Oh no, don't you dare think you can start tugging me as well. Storm sat down.

Jessie crossed her arms and sighed, her cheeks turning red. Some of her lightning smell crept back, confused and frustrated. If only humans knew the language of the skies so he could talk to her, it would make things a lot easier. Storm resolved to speak with Odin about it when the Hunt returned.

The humans all shuffled closer into a circle, urging their dogs to follow. Some of them did, the Great Dane taking a few steps forward, then lying down again.

'Storm, sit,' Fuzzy-Lady said.

He was already sitting. What more did she want?

Nothing, apparently. The Fuzzy-Lady bent to scratch him behind his ears. 'Good boy, Storm.'

Lady, you are insane. But what was the use in telling her that? She couldn't understand a single word he was saying. But then she dug in her fuzzy pocket and offered him something crunchy. He'd thought the meaty chunks were delicious, but this tasted of a whole herd of cattle squashed down into one crispy morsel. Storm snapped it up. Maybe he wouldn't smite her for her insolence just yet. She was human and stupid, after all. She didn't know any better.

The dogs around him yapped, trying to get their own crunchy treats.

Wait your turn, Storm growled, his shadow growing for a moment. The Great Dane whined and shrank back.

Fuzzy-Lady handed Storm's leash back to Jessie. 'Well,' she said with a nervous laugh, 'let's get started. Everyone, tell your dogs to sit.'

How was this supposed to teach the humans to obey?

Unless . . .

No, it was too horrible to contemplate.

Storm stood up in alarm.

'Sit, Storm,' Jessie said, bending and gently pushing him down.

Storm's bottom sank to the floor. Along with the last shreds of his dignity.

I find if you ignore the humans for long enough they give you the treats anyway, a female terrier said, her tail wagging nervously.

Storm twisted his head, feeling the tug of the leash on his collar. *Quiz night?* he said.

The Great Dane avoided his gaze.

This was no game: humans actually believed they were in charge. The events of the past week suddenly made an awful kind of sense. Jessie's father shutting him in the back room . . . Jessie scolding him for chasing next door's cat . . .

How could this be? Jessie was only a child; she wasn't even in charge of her own life. Storm had seen her leave the house resentfully to go to somewhere called 'school'. Even her father, who was a grown man, couldn't command the clouds, or even the smallest patch of earth beneath his feet.

It makes them feel better, the yellow Labrador said, noticing Storm's confusion. *The world is vast*

and they are little. It frightens them. Just do what the humans want and they'll be happy and feed you. It's how things work.

'Sit, Buttercup,' the Labrador's human said. He sat back and looked up at his human servant adoringly, until the lady gave him a treat. His tail thumped.

This is slavery, Storm said. He still couldn't believe the dogs would go along with this so easily. Didn't they know they were descended from wolves? Where was their pride, their self-respect? Storm let out a whimper.

Oh, don't be so dramatic, the Labrador said, standing up again. *It's an exchange. Follow a few simple instructions and the humans think you're some kind of genius and feed you treats. You should try it.*

'Buttercup, sit,' the Labrador's human said.

The Labrador sat down. The human squealed. Two of the other humans applauded.

'Well done,' Fuzzy-Lady said, and Storm wasn't sure whether she was talking to the Labrador or his human. They both seemed equally pleased.

Jessie shook Storm's leash. 'Storm, sit.'

Storm fixed her with a stare. *You sit. I'm quite comfortable standing.*

Jessie's eyes became pleading. 'Storm, please sit down.'

Her scent became anxious and she sounded like

she was about to cry. Storm suddenly found that he didn't want that.

He was a stormhound. Humans should obey him, not the other way round. On the other hand, she'd said 'please'. Maybe it was all right to obey a request – especially when Jessie had tried so hard to please him.

Oh, all right, then. Storm sat down and wagged his tail.

The sudden change that came over Jessie's face was worth thunder and lightning. The threat of tears vanished and she gave a big grin, her scent lighting up the hall. 'Did you see that?' she shouted.

The Labrador's human laughed. 'He was waiting for you to ask politely. Try it again.'

'Storm,' Jessie said, 'please would you mind standing up?'

Storm waited a moment to build up suspense before he stood. *I'm only doing this to make you look good in front of the other humans. I hope you appreciate it.*

She did, he could tell. Her usually pale face flushed with pleasure.

'You've got a knack for this,' the Labrador's lady said.

She's got a knack for saying words?

'Sit,' Jessie said.

Storm wondered whether to do it this time.

121

'Sit, please,' Jessie said, her face full of admiration. He sat down.

'Here,' Fuzzy-Lady said, taking the leash back. 'Let me try. Storm, please stand up.'

Storm looked at her and, very deliberately, he lay down.

Jessie laughed. 'It's like he did that on purpose.'

You bet I did.

And then the door opened, letting in a gust of rain and three men in overcoats.

CHAPTER 19

Storm flattened himself to the floor. Something was very wrong with these men. They smelled normal enough at first sniff, but something else lurked beneath the combination of human, wet clothes, cheese and onion. The unmistakeable whiff of danger.

'What are *they* doing here?' Jessie muttered.

Storm smelled the tension rising inside her, her sharp lightning-scent beginning to crackle.

Fuzzy-Lady's face creased in annoyance. She strode to the door, blocking the intruders from coming any closer. 'Can I help you, gentlemen?'

The tallest of the three took off his hat. 'I do beg your pardon. I am Professor Utterby from Bangor University, and these are my colleagues, Professors Ryston and Nuffield. We were taking an after-dinner stroll when it began to rain rather heavily and we were forced to head for the nearest shelter. Here,' he added, gesturing around in case Fuzzy-Lady hadn't understood.

He'd said 'Professors'! These must be the people

Jessie had talked about yesterday with the Not-Boy.

Jessie nudged Storm behind her. 'Stay,' she murmured. She couldn't hope to protect him with her puny human body, but she was trying anyway. Storm felt pride surge through him and a snarl rose in his chest. His hair prickled.

Careful, young one, the Great Dane growled. *Don't start a fight you can't win.*

'That's a very large dog,' Professor Ryston said, his gaze snapping to the Great Dane. 'When did you acquire him?'

'I am in the middle of teaching a class,' said Fuzzy-Lady, putting her hands on her hips. 'If you could kindly . . .'

Professor Utterby tossed something that looked like soot into the air. 'Sit,' he said. 'The rest of you, stay.'

Fuzzy-Lady paused, her mouth opening, then she sat down on the floor and crossed her legs. The other humans all stood as if they'd been frozen – even Jessie.

Storm's ears flattened. This was the worst kind of magic, smelling of ancient graves and desolate mountainsides. He tugged at Jessie's leash, but she didn't move.

The three professors moved forward. Storm felt a creeping compulsion to howl, to spill his shadow across the hall and send these three intruders running for their lives. He tensed, feeling all his hair stand on end as the professors walked towards the Great Dane.

Begone, and take your magic with you! Storm snarled. Too late he remembered the cat's warning about keeping his magic hidden. It was too late now, anyway; his shadow was halfway across the floor

Professor Utterby paused mid-stride and started to turn. But then the sharp, bright smell of lightning cut through the cold hall.

'Storm, stay,' Jessie said.

Storm looked up at her in surprise. She'd been frozen a moment ago. How had she broken free?

The scent of dark magic fled, leaving a clear patch where Storm could breathe freely. His shadow settled back down, puppy-sized again.

Jessie had magic! Only a little, and clearly unused and untrained. She didn't seem to realize it herself. The professors weren't looking at him now – they were all staring at Jessie.

'You were in chemistry yesterday,' Professor Utterby said. 'How long have you had this dog?'

Jessie drew in an unsteady breath. 'A few months. We got him back home, in London.'

She'd lied. *Well done, Jessie.* Storm felt Jessie trembling. He crouched, ready to leap at the man. His shadow pulsed like lightning about to break forth from a cloud. He was a stormhound, not a terrified pup, and Jessie was only a child. It was up to him to protect her.

Professor Utterby's gaze shot back to him as the door opened again and the Not-Boy walked in.

Like a thread snapping, the spell that held the humans broke. The Great Dane growled. His voice was echoed by the Labrador. Some of the other dogs took the chance to snap up crunchy treats from the floor, chewing loudly.

Fuzzy-Lady scrambled up, her scent a mixture of confusion and fear, as if some part of her tiny human mind was aware of what had just happened. 'You need to leave,' she said. 'You can't come in here and disrupt the class.'

Professor Utterby looked as if he were about to argue, but then he nodded curtly. 'I believe the rain is easing. We'll be on our way. I will see you in class tomorrow, Miss Price. Please forget we were ever here.' He stalked out, followed by Ryston and Nuffield.

The Not-Boy jigged from foot to foot. 'See you tomorrow,' he said to Jessie, and ran out.

Did you see that? Storm barked happily. *We ran them all off without even trying. They won't come again in a hurry. Can I have another of those crunchy things?*

Jessie shook her head, her scent a mix of lightning and worry. 'Heel, Storm,' she said, and while

Storm was still wondering what that was supposed to mean, she ran after the Not-Boy.

He couldn't have gone far, but the street was empty – except for the flash of a rabbit or hare, tearing behind a hedge.

CHAPTER 20

David bounded away, his ears and tail twitching, the sudden rush of all his senses coming into focus, making him momentarily dizzy. He heard Jessie shouting his name, but he didn't stop. He shouldn't have dragged her into this in the first place. And now the professors had noticed her.

He kept running, his hare legs carrying him quickly until he reached the park by the bus station and the narrow river. An orange-and-black motorbike stood, leaning against a tree. David glanced around to make sure he was alone, then drew in a shuddering breath and turned back into a boy.

'Auntie Ceridwen?'

She stepped out from behind the tree. The look in her eyes made David want to tuck his tail into his legs and bolt for the mountains. But he didn't have a tail at the moment, or the option of bolting anyway. He curled his fingers into his palms to stop his hands from shaking.

Ceridwen growled at the back of her throat. 'What

exactly do you think you're doing?'

David picked at a thread on his trousers. 'I was following the professors. Like you told me to, remember?'

'Don't cheek me. I told you to keep an eye on things from a distance and make sure they didn't see you. Your friend was shouting after you, you know.'

'I heard her.' David shoved his hands into his pockets angrily. 'What's wrong with making a friend? Just because you like being on your own all the time, it doesn't mean I have to do the same.'

'How much does she know?' Ceridwen asked.

Of course, that was all his aunt really cared about: making sure their various secrets were kept. 'Nothing,' David said. Ceridwen stared at him disbelievingly and he felt colour rise to his cheeks. 'I already told you. She's guessed there's something up with the professors, but she has no idea what's going on. She thinks the profs are bank robbers or something.'

He hated lying to his aunt, but she had ways of meddling with people's memories if she thought they knew too much. He attempted a smile. 'She wouldn't believe me even if I told her – which I'm not going to do.'

That was true enough. No one would ever believe him. Magic existed. His aunt policed it out of family duty. David wasn't really a boy, but a hare who could change shape, and the professors were searching for some sort of magical artefact, probably powerful and dangerous.

His aunt started to walk, assuming he'd follow. He should take off in the other direction: that'd teach her.

'This is because you still haven't found out what the professors are looking for, isn't it?' he said, following her. 'It's not my fault, so don't take it out on me.' His aunt turned her head to glare at him and he hunched his shoulders. 'Sorry.'

Ceridwen slowed and sighed. 'Morfran, I know this isn't always easy, but I'm not making up these rules to annoy you. I'm trying to protect you. Magic and mortals are like oil and water. They don't mix.'

David took his hands out of his pockets and ran one through his hair, feeling the notch in his ear. 'They could, though, couldn't they? I'm a mix.'

'And what would your human friend say if she knew?' Ceridwen asked. 'Just because you can walk on two legs, it doesn't make you one of them.' She put a hand on his shoulder. 'Don't underestimate yourself, Morfran. When I rescued you, I did it because I felt sorry for you – an injured baby, clinging to life. I didn't think you'd even survive, but you surprised me. You proved to be far stronger than you looked.'

'And you taught me magic,' David said. She could have kept him as a pet, but instead she'd taught him to draw power from the earth, just like the ancient enchanters had done. She'd given him consciousness and the ability to change shape, so now he was more boy than hare.

The first stars were appearing over the mountains. David dropped his gaze from them. He should be grateful – and he was. It was just that sometimes he wished he could be David the boy instead of Morfran the . . . whatever he was.

'I made an exception for you because I could see you were special,' Ceridwen said, as if reading his mind. 'But magic must be contained. It should never have entered this world in the first place.'

'That wasn't your fault,' David said.

Ceridwen sighed. 'I know. But I must bear the responsibility for it. There are always people like the professors trying to pull magic out of its proper place. If I leave them to it, before we know it they'll be summoning monsters from the Otherworld and no one will be safe.'

Monsters from the Otherworld.

David stopped still. His aunt's words bounced in his head, colliding with all his jumbled thoughts: the professors searching the mountains, Professor Nuffield talking about the Wild Hunt. And, just now, he'd been afraid the professors had followed Jessie into the dog class, but they hadn't been looking for her at all.

'Dogs,' he said, his voice barely a whisper. *If*

Odin was around today, you might see a giant dog prowling in the mountains, Professor Nuffield had said. David closed his fingers into his palms, his nails digging in. 'They're not hunting for a magical artefact, they're looking for a dog – one of Odin's dogs, a hound of the Wild Hunt.'

He risked a glance at his aunt, trying to read her expression. He hoped she'd be pleased he'd worked it out. But as realization slowly crossed her face – the realization that he was right – she turned white.

'No,' she said. 'Stormhounds are terrible creatures. Monsters who live only for the pleasure of hunting and destroying. If there was a stormhound here, it would kill everything in its path – animals, birds, people.'

David's heart thumped. The shadows along the river looked suddenly threatening, as if each one might contain a stormhound getting ready to pounce.

'Why would the professors want a stormhound?' he asked. 'I mean, if they're that dangerous?'

'Because they are created from magic. Their blood, bones, hair – every part of them – can be used in magic spells. Even the tears of a stormhound – if such a creature could ever cry – are said to heal all injuries. Just think of what the professors could do with that sort of power.'

David thought, and his mind led him in all sorts of unpleasant directions. He wrapped his arms around himself and shivered. 'Friday the seventh on Mount

Skirrid. That's what was written on the map in the professors' staffroom. Is that where the stormhound will be?'

'Or where they're planning to kill it.' Ceridwen put a hand on his shoulder, her eyes like stone. 'I'm here, remember, and it's my job to protect you from this sort of thing. Tonight, I'll renew our defence charms and I'll cast a confusion spell over the town. That should distract the professors for a little while. We must use that time to find the stormhound and dispose of it. Before the professors find it, before it can do any harm.'

David knew his aunt didn't like casting that much magic. This must be really serious.

'You'll need to end your friendship with the mortal girl too,' Ceridwen said.

David's heart dropped. 'Jessie's not my . . .' He started to protest, but even as he spoke, the words felt wrong. He looked down at his feet. 'I like her – she's different.' She was too. She'd seen through Ceridwen's disguise spells and she seemed immune to the professors' magic. An image rose into his mind: Jessie facing down his aunt, her dog growling like a storm cloud at her feet.

He pushed the image aside. If Jessie had any magic, she didn't know about it, and it was better to keep it that way. He knew what Ceridwen did to people if she thought they were misusing magic. 'You keep telling me I should behave like a human,' he muttered, 'and humans have friends.'

'And you're going to get your friend killed if you drag her into this,' Ceridwen said harshly. 'Have you considered that?'

No, of course he hadn't. David squashed the ugly swell of guilt inside him. 'I didn't drag Jessie into anything. She kept asking questions. Was I supposed to ignore her?'

His aunt sighed. 'Maybe it was a mistake to send you into that school on your own. I thought you could handle it. I keep forgetting how young you are.'

Now he felt doubly guilty – for putting Jessie in danger and for letting his aunt down. David kicked at the grass. 'All right. Let me have one more day in school and I'll tell Jessie I can't be friends with her.'

'You, wanting to go to school? You'll be wanting to do homework and sit exams next.' She smiled suddenly. 'Come on. I'll race you home.'

The air shimmered and the two people vanished. Seconds later, two white hares, one smaller and with a notched ear, bounded along the street in the direction of the river.

CHAPTER 21

What was the point of being a stormhound if you were stuck in a house all day? Storm should be out and about, prowling the streets and looking for dark magic, not shut indoors while the humans went about their mysterious work and school tasks. Jessie ought to study faster so she could come home early and get on with more important tasks – such as attending to a bored stormhound.

He was hungry too. He'd refused breakfast this morning in an attempt to show Jessie something was wrong with the world. It had worked, but not in the way he'd expected. Jessie's Dad had threatened the vet again, and he'd thrown the uneaten meaty chunks into a metal bin which was full of so much unappetizing rubbish that Storm had left them alone. He was getting soft: he'd eaten far worse than that in Odin's halls.

Come to think of it, Odin's hunters didn't pay their dogs half the attention Storm got from Jessie, Ben and their Dad, or care when the hounds were sick. Storm would have to have a word with Odin about that when he got back.

Sighing, he stood up and padded to the kitchen – Jessie's Dad had given up locking him in the back room, saying Storm was scratching the door to pieces, which was an exaggeration, but not completely untrue, though it was entirely the fault of the humans for putting a door in the way of where he wanted to go.

Next-door's cat was sitting right outside the back door. Storm pawed at the glass. *Hey, cat, how do you open this?*

The cat flicked her paw over her ears. *You don't. There'll be a key somewhere, most likely, but if I were you I'd stay where you are today. It's not safe out.*

Storm's hair prickled. The cat was outside. Did she think she was braver and stronger than he was? *Insolent animal*, he growled. *I do not fear humans, even those who use magic.*

I thought you wouldn't. The cat began cleaning her tabby fur. *But you should be afraid. You're going to get yourself into trouble, charging off after them. You keep forgetting you're only a puppy here.*

As if he could forget that. He remembered how he'd been ready to leap at the three professors last night, to teach them the folly of messing with Otherworld magic, his shadow pulsing while his puppy body had trembled pathetically. And the dark magician had looked at him and dismissed him. He'd thought his smallness was his greatest weakness in this world. What if it was the only thing that was preventing the hunters from finding him?

What about the Not-Boy? he asked, less certainly. Jessie seemed to like him, and he hadn't done anything to hurt her yet, unlike the Mum-Person.

The cat wiped a paw across her ear. *Let him walk about on two legs if it makes him happy. I don't think he's a threat.*

That's not good enough. This place is filling up with magic. We must do something. Storm jumped up at the back door, trying to grab the handle with his teeth. All he managed to do was slide down the glass and land in a heap.

After he'd done it the third time, the cat stopped washing. *Tell you what. I'll go and spy out the neighbourhood. You wait here and I'll bring you word of what's happening.*

Storm picked himself up and shook himself. *Why would you do that?*

Because I'm curious too. And I'm getting tired of you complaining that you don't know anything. Do you want me to go or not?

Storm considered. *This won't mean we're partners, or friends or anything, will it?*

Of course not. What do you take me for? I am a cat; you are a creature of the Otherworld. And, even

if you weren't, you'd still be a dog. The cat hissed to show what she thought of dogs.

Storm wagged his tail at her. *Well, then, I suppose it can't hurt. I give you leave to depart.*

I resent that, the cat said, and walked away, flicking her tail. Storm watched her go, sighed and went upstairs to find some towels to chew.

The cat didn't appear again all morning. Jessie came home as usual in the middle of the day, and because Storm didn't want her to worry unduly (never mind that he was hungry, and the meaty chunks smelled delicious), he wolfed down a whole bowl of food and pawed at her leg until she gave him more. Jessie hugged him.

'Good boy, Storm. Well done.'

It's not exactly a heroic achievement to eat when you're hungry, you know. Storm gave her a quick lick anyway, and escorted her to the front door when it was time for her to go back to school. Then he sat and waited.

Finally, as the sun dipped behind the mountains, Storm saw tabby fur slinking over the fence between the houses. He raced to the back door, thought better of it, and sat under the kitchen table, pretending he hadn't noticed her.

Dog! Nutmeg yowled. *Beware!*

Storm leaped to his feet, barking. *Beware of what?*

Magic. Dark magic. She dashed away over the fence to her own garden.

Where is Jessie? Storm barked after her. If anything had happened to her, he didn't care if he was the size of a puppy – he'd tear those professors apart.

CHAPTER 22

'Storm!' Jessie called, opening the front door. She was glad to be home. The professors hadn't shown up at school today, and David had arrived late, looking red-eyed with tiredness. He'd refused to say a word about what had happened last night at the obedience class, and when she'd invited him back for tea again she thought he was going to say 'no', but he'd suddenly changed his mind. And now he loitered behind her on the pavement, looking like he was about to change his mind again.

Storm dashed out to meet her, his tail wagging frantically.

Jessie laughed. 'Down, Storm. We'll take you for a walk in a minute.'

'Actually, I think it might rain,' David said. 'You should stay in tonight, and keep the doors and windows locked.'

'Why? This is Abergavenny, remember? The most dangerous thing that's happened was when Mrs Williams yelled at us because Storm chased her cat.'

David glanced about, looking nervous.

'Have you argued with your aunt again?' Jessie asked him.

'Sort of.' He let out a breath. 'Listen, there's something I need to tell you.'

Finally! Jessie folded her arms and stared at him. 'You can start with exactly what's going on here. Why are the professors so interested in other people's dogs? Who is your aunt really?'

But then another voice drifted down the street.

'I hate school!' Ben shouted.

They both turned. Jessie ran out on to the pavement and saw Ben marching towards her.

'What's wrong?' she asked.

'Nothing.' He flung his school bag into the house, then tore off his coat and threw that too. 'I hate this town. I hate Wales. I want to go home.'

Jessie tried to hug him but he pushed her away.

'This doesn't sound like nothing,' she said. It was the kind of thing Mum would say. Ben's eyes filled with tears. He turned away from her, wiping his face on his sleeve. 'Some of the kids at school were saying things, that's all. They said the reason we don't live with Mum is because she doesn't want us.' He sniffed loudly.

Something inside Jessie curled up tight. She'd thought Ben was getting on all right at his new school. But then she hadn't really been paying attention this week and she should have. She was supposed be looking after Ben. Storm licked her hand as she crouched down in front of her brother.

'Ben, she said. 'You know Mum would have us if she had space. And Dad wants us too, don't forget.'

'She's right,' David said. 'You've got two people who want you, in two different places. That makes you twice as lucky as those other kids. They're just jealous.'

Storm dashed into the house and emerged seconds later, carrying his lead. Jessie laughed, and found it eased the ache inside her.

'Why don't you hold Storm's lead today?' she asked. 'David, are you coming? You wanted to tell me something, remember?'

He glanced at Ben and shook his head. 'It'll keep. I'll come with you, though, just in case.'

Just in case of what? But David was already walking on ahead. He clearly didn't want to talk to her in front of Ben. Sighing, Jessie locked the front door and followed with Ben, and Storm tugging excitedly between them.

They headed to the castle and sat down on one of the humps of grass, their backs against a wall. Jessie unclipped Storm's lead. Normally he'd have torn off in pursuit of squirrels, but today he sat down a few paces away, watching them. As if he were on guard duty.

A few cold splashes of rain fell.

Ben heaved a sigh. 'I hate this place. It's always raining. I want to go home to London.'

Jessie wished she knew what to say to him. She wanted to go back to London too, but she didn't want to leave Storm. And, even if they did go back, would it feel like home without Dad there? She pulled out a piece of paper and a pen and began to draw the scene around her: the broken walls of the castle, the green spike of the market tower that seemed to be visible from everywhere. It was a good scene to draw, she had to admit that. She added a hare running across the grass and then a second one alongside it. She didn't know why: it just felt right.

David stretched his arms out over his head. 'I've been all over the world, and I can tell you, this is a good place. The mountains feel friendly, as if they're looking after the town. And you can't say you don't like the castle. Everyone loves castles.'

'They're all right,' Ben said grudgingly.

David pulled a tuft of grass out of the wall. 'They're better than all right. Put your hands here, both of you.'

Jessie put down her pen and spread her fingers over the stones. Even Storm came over and sniffed at the wall.

'I can't feel anything,' Ben said.

David grinned. 'No, but think of all the people who've put their hands exactly where yours are now.'

'Yuck.' Ben wiped his hand on his trousers, but he was smiling.

They sat for a while longer, until the castle gates were ready to be closed for the evening. As they left the grounds, Jessie saw a man hurrying towards them, holding a dog's lead.

Storm yapped. It was Viking's owner – the Great Dane from the obedience class.

'Have you seen Viking?' he asked. 'I was taking him for a walk and he just disappeared. I can't find him anywhere.'

CHAPTER 23

Danger! Dark magic. The cat had said so.

Storm stood still, his ears quivering. He could smell something else now — so faint he'd missed it at first. Something ancient and cold.

He barked and tugged hard on his leash.

'We'll help you look,' Jessie said. 'Storm, heel.'

Hurry up, then.

The scent of magic came in patches, here and there, leading across the grass back into town. Storm pulled harder on the leash, making Jessie walk faster. Finally he'd found a use for the silly thing, making Jessie follow him.

Viking's human hurried behind with the Not-Boy.

And what was wrong with the Not-Boy all of a sudden? He'd seemed nervous before, but now he smelled overwhelmingly of fear and he kept twisting his head from side to side, staring at everything.

'I've already checked the High Street,' Viking's human said as they came within sight of the shops. 'I was going to try the river.'

145

He could if he wanted, but the trail didn't point towards the river. Storm headed determinedly in the other direction where the sparks of dark magic seemed strongest.

Aha! Here was Viking's smell: a big patch of it, and then the metal stink of one of those loathsome cars. He paused to give it a good sniff, then led the humans on. This was not quite a Wild Hunt – more a disorderly one, with Jessie, Ben, the Not-Boy and Viking's human getting in each other's way behind him – but his blood buzzed with anticipation.

He was Storm of Odin, striding down the High Street.

He was Storm of Odin, with rain in his fur and his senses alive.

He was Storm of Odin, sitting down at the pedestrian crossing waiting for the lights to change.

And then, sometime later, the smell of magic was overtaken by a flood of Great Dane. Storm paused, feeling his hair rise on end, the collar tugging at his neck.

There!

There, where the end of a black tail poked out from underneath a hedge. The humans didn't even see it until Storm dragged Jessie closer and then the Not-Boy shouted.

The dog was lying on his side, not moving. Ben took a step back. 'Is he . . . ?'

Storm nudged the inert body with his nose. *Get up, will you? You're scaring the humans.* Viking didn't move. Storm nipped him sharply on the ear. *I know you're alive. I am Storm of Odin, stormhound of the Wild Hunt, and you will do as I say. Get up!*

For a moment he felt huge again. His shadow spread out around him, swallowing the pavement. Viking stirred, gave a Great Dane-sized cough, and lifted his head.

'He's alive!' Ben shouted.

Viking's human dropped to his knees, running his hands over the dog, babbling questions Viking couldn't understand. Storm wriggled in under his arms.

What happened to you? You stink of magic. Was it the professors?

Viking lowered his head to the pavement. *I don't remember. They lit tiny fires on sticks that smelled funny.*

Candles, probably. Odin's halls were full of them. *You must remember something*, Storm growled.

They said I wasn't the dog they were looking for. Viking burrowed his head into his human's clothes. For such a big dog, he was quite pathetic.

'I'll take him straight to the vet,' Viking's human said. 'Can you watch him for a minute while I get my car?'

He was back two minutes later. Viking was on his

feet by then, stumbling unsteadily.

Storm sniffed Viking's nose. The smell of magic was already fading. Some meaty chunks and a night curled by the fire, and he'd be fine.

Take care, little one, the Great Dane said as his human helped him into the car and jumped into the front.

Storm watched the car drive away.

I am not a little one. I am a . . .

He heard a sound behind and turned to see the Not-Boy staring at him, his eyes completely round in his pale face.

Storm shook his head and tried to look innocent and puppyish, but it was too late. The Not-Boy had seen his shadow grow. He'd guessed what Storm was, and the knowledge had terrified him.

'David?' Jessie asked, reaching out to him in concern. 'Will you please tell me what's going on? Tell me the truth.'

The Not-Boy shoved her hand aside. 'I can't be your friend,' he said. 'That's what I was going to tell you before. I'll be leaving soon and I've got other things to do. I don't have time to hang around with you. Just . . . just stay away from the professors and you'll be fine.'

He turned and walked away from them, then he started to run.

'David!' Jessie shouted. The Not-Boy didn't stop.

Jessie crumpled in surprise. Storm stood in front of her, his tail wagging against her legs.

That's right, coward, you can keep running. We don't need you.

CHAPTER 24

'Your friend is weird,' Ben said as the three of them made their way home.

Everything was weird, thought Jessie. Viking hadn't just run off – he'd looked ill. And David had seemed afraid. What else did he know that he wasn't telling her? It didn't matter now, she supposed. She should have believed him the first time he'd said he didn't make friends. She'd just wasted a whole week talking to him – and she couldn't believe she'd helped him break into the professors' staffroom yesterday.

Dad came running the moment they opened the door of the house.

'Where have you two been? Why didn't you answer your phones?'

Jessie saw the missed messages. 'Sorry,' she said. 'Someone lost his dog and we were helping to look. You knew we'd be out with Storm, though.'

'I assumed you were, yes, but I didn't know. You should have left a message.' He gave a strained smile. 'I worry about you both, you know.'

If that was supposed to make her feel better, it didn't work. She already had to try to make sure Ben didn't get upset. Now she had to keep Dad from worrying too.

Storm stopped by the hall table and looked up at the telephone. It rang.

'It's like he knew!' Ben laughed.

Of course he hadn't. How could he?

Jessie picked the phone up. 'Hello?'

'Hello, Lightning Bug,' Mum said.

Straight away the world felt better, as if all the bits that were in the wrong places had been put back where they belonged.

It's Mum, Jessie mouthed at Ben and Dad.

Dad nodded, mimed making a drink and walked off to the kitchen. Ben tried to grab the phone out of Jessie's hand and she fended him off.

'Wait your turn. Mum, we just took Storm for a walk and we helped find a missing dog. I think he might be ill.'

'Who, Storm?'

'No, the other dog. He looked all funny. His owner's taken him to the vet. Are you coming to visit this weekend?'

'I'm afraid I can't,' Mum said. 'I've got to work. But I will visit soon. I'll talk to your dad about it later. And . . .' she added as Ben pressed his head against Jessie's so he could hear, 'I have some good news.'

151

Jessie's heart jumped.

'Mum's coming to live with us!' Ben shouted.

'I'm afraid not, Lightning Bug.' Mum's voice sounded tight, worried.

The phone started to feel slippery in Jessie's hand. She wiped her palm on her trouser leg. 'Ben, you can have your turn in a minute,' she said, taking the phone into the front room and closing the door, shutting Ben and Storm out. 'What's happened?' she asked. 'You haven't got a boyfriend, have you?'

She hadn't realized how much she'd worried about that until the words were out. Her eyes burned with tears. 'Because it's all right if you have,' she said. 'I mean, Ben will probably be upset at first, but he'll get used to it . . .' It was no good. All the words she wanted to say bundled up in her throat and she couldn't get them out.

Mum laughed. 'It's nothing like that.' She seemed to realize this was something serious and she paused. 'Jessie, I promise if that ever happens I'll tell you. Are you OK?'

Jessie wiped her eyes. 'Yes. It's been a strange day, that's all. What's your news?'

'I'm moving house,' Mum said.

Jessie didn't know what to say. Of all the things Mum might have told her, Jessie wouldn't have guessed that. She gripped the phone, listening to the sound of her own breathing. 'But why?'

'Because I need somewhere bigger, of course,' Mum said. 'I've found a flat, not too far from where I am now. It's got two bedrooms. You and Ben will have your own space when you visit. You'll have to share if you come together, but you can take it in turns too, whichever you prefer. You can spend the whole school holidays with me if you like.'

She was talking too fast, cramming words together without giving Jessie a chance to answer. 'You can decorate the room yourselves,' she said, 'and choose whatever furniture you want. It'll be yours. You'll be able to have your friends round – we can have a welcome party if you like.'

'What about Storm?' Jessie broke in. 'Can I bring him?'

Mum paused and sighed. 'I don't know, Lightning Bug.' The excitement drained from her voice and she sounded tired now. She'd wanted them to be happy about the news.

'It doesn't matter,' Jessie said.

'No, it does. Of course you have to bring Storm. Maybe my allergy won't be so bad. We can try it and see. We'll sort the details out later. The important thing is you and Ben can live with me part of the time. If you want to, of course,' she added. Her voice wobbled, just a little.

Jessie gripped the phone hard. 'Of course I want to. It's just . . .' She felt suddenly exhausted, as if

Mum, Dad, Ben – all of it – was a huge weight and she couldn't carry it any longer. 'Ben's waiting to talk to you,' she said. 'You should tell him the news. Bye, Mum.'

She ran back into the hall, ignoring Mum's voice asking her to wait and pushed the phone at Ben.

'Hi, Mum,' Ben said. 'Abergavenny's got a castle. When are you coming to visit?'

'What do you want for dinner?' Dad asked, coming out of the kitchen. His face creased in worry.

'You knew about this, didn't you?' Jessie asked.

He looked down, avoiding her gaze. 'Only for a little while. Mum wanted to tell you herself.'

'We can stay with you?' Ben shouted into the phone. 'Fantastic! Bags me first.'

Dad wrapped his arms round Jessie's shoulders. 'I know things are all a bit strange and difficult right now, but your mum loves you. We're still a family.'

A family split across hundreds of miles, with her and Ben travelling back and forth, never quite belonging in either place. She squirmed free. 'I've got homework to do.'

Storm followed Jessie upstairs. He wasn't really supposed to go in the bedrooms, but Jessie's Dad didn't call him back so he nosed the bedroom door open and padded through.

Jessie was lying on her bed, staring up at the

ceiling. Storm climbed up next to her and she wriggled up to make room for him. He lay down against her with a sigh. He wanted to tell her there were more important things happening than the Mum-Person keeping secrets or Dad being cross – things like dark magicians and Not-Boys – but he knew she couldn't understand him. And, anyway, he had the feeling that even if Jessie did know the truth, the things that happened in this little house would still be more important to her.

Jessie curled tighter around him. 'I used to wish for a dog all the time,' she said. 'I wanted a puppy – a white one with ears that stood up like triangles. And a little black nose.' She opened her eyes, blinking against Storm's dark fur. 'You know, if Mum and Dad hadn't split up, we wouldn't have moved here and I wouldn't have found you.'

Storm sniffed her chin. Her smell was sharp, full of tears and angry lightning. He licked Jessie on the cheek, tasting salt. He knew how she must be feeling. Falling to earth hadn't been good, but some of it was tolerable. The meaty chunks, for example, and the warmth of a blanket at night. And Jessie herself.

Jessie sniffed and brushed away tears. 'You're a good dog, Storm.'

No, he wasn't. He was Storm of Odin, who ran with the Wild Hunt and tore the night apart for the joy of it. He was everything that was untamed and free.

Humans and their little lives were over in an instant and none of them should matter to him.

But, here and now, he was Storm, licking salty tears off his human's face as she cried.

CHAPTER 25

David should have gone straight back to the house he and Ceridwen were renting by the river, but he couldn't make himself do it. He walked along the High Street instead, looking in the windows of shops that were shut for the day while the sky grew steadily darker.

It was Storm.

The stormhound – the great, slavering monster his aunt was so worried about. *Storm.* How hadn't he realized straight away? That uneasy prickling that seemed to fill his whole body when Storm was around. He'd put it down to his natural unease around dogs. And then there'd been the way the puppy was always looking at him as if it understood every word he said. But David hadn't been looking for a stormhound then, and he'd wanted Jessie to like him, and . . .

No, he should have known. David shuddered, remembering the sight of Storm's shadow spread monstrously large on the pavement, and the hound's voice rumbling through his mind like thunder.

He couldn't hide from the fact any longer, no matter how he wished it wasn't true. The stormhound was Storm.

What was he going to do?

A creature of the Otherworld. A monster, filled with unimaginable power. David pictured the black puppy twining himself protectively around Jessie's legs, growling his little puppy growl; Storm chasing squirrels in the castle grounds, tugging Jessie along in the hunt to find Viking. Those weren't the actions of a monster. Well, the squirrels might disagree, but it wasn't as if Storm had climbed the tree after them.

He should tell Ceridwen and let her decide what to do.

But he had seen how Jessie had stood between the professors and Storm at the obedience class, and he could imagine too clearly what Jessie would do if Ceridwen tried to take Storm from her. There were any number of things Ceridwen could do in return – from enchanting Jessie so she'd forget everything, to putting her to sleep for a year. And she'd do it believing it was the right thing.

David groaned. He'd never felt this torn before.

'Morfran!' a familiar voice snapped.

David turned, forcing himself to smile.

'Where have you been?' Ceridwen asked. 'I told you to come straight home from school. It's not safe to be outside with a stormhound on the loose.'

She sounded for a moment as if David were a real boy and she were his real aunt, worrying about him. David should have laughed, but inside he felt a tight pain in his chest.

'You're outside,' he pointed out.

'I know what I'm doing.' She stretched as if trying to ease pains out of her shoulders. 'I've spent the day hunting. Once or twice I thought I caught the scent of the creature, but never for long, and never enough to track it to its lair.'

She didn't know about Storm. David tried not to let his relief show on his face. He pushed his hands in his pockets to stop them from trembling. 'Auntie Ceridwen,' he said. 'You know you said we had to dispose of the stormhound? You meant . . .'

'Kill it,' she said, nodding. 'It's the only thing we can do.'

David felt cold. 'But what if it isn't? What if the stormhound isn't as bad as you think? Maybe that's why we can't find it, because we've all been looking for a monster. What if it's more like a normal dog, for example? A puppy.'

Ceridwen's gaze sharpened. 'If you have something to say, Morfran . . .'

'No. I'm just trying to think of all the options. Even if it *is* just a harmless puppy, you'll still kill it?'

'There's no such thing as a harmless stormhound,' Ceridwen said, frowning. 'This is a creature from

159

the Otherworld. It might manage to disguise its true nature for a little while, though I fail to see why it would, but it is still the same inside. So, yes, I will do what's necessary.'

'And what about Odin?' David asked. 'What about the Wild Hunt?' he said, his voice rising angrily. 'If they come looking for their missing hound and you've killed it—'

'Odin is bound by the rules, as we are,' Ceridwen said. 'In the mortal world, the stormhound is outside his protection – and if Odin has a problem with that, he can challenge me and we'll fight it out, but it won't come to that.' She smiled thinly. 'Go on indoors now. I'll continue the search.'

She walked away, then stopped sharply. 'Morfran?'

David's heart jumped.

'Your friend,' Ceridwen said. 'The girl. That's all finished?'

David nodded. 'I won't speak to her again.'

'Good. And thank you.'

David watched her go, shivering slightly as her words echoed in his head. *The stormhound might disguise its true nature for a while, but it's still the same inside.*

Did she think the same of him too? He'd begun life as a hare, and look at him now. He didn't feel quite human inside, but he didn't feel like a hare either, neither one thing nor the other. And if that had happened to him, could the same thing happen to a stormhound?

For the first time in many years David wished he was an ordinary hare so he didn't have to worry about any of this.

He walked in the direction of the river, but instead of turning aside to the house he kept walking, away from the town until the road widened and houses gave way to fields. Then he began to run, heading towards the low mountain peaks beyond the town. At some point he found himself running on four legs and he knew he'd changed shape without noticing.

David didn't run far, only to a split in the road where sheep were grazing on the stubby grass. He paused and nibbled at a yellow stalk, trying to pretend he still liked the taste.

Baaaa!

A large, black-faced ewe stood behind him. The hare spat out grass. *Sorry. Not in the mood to talk.*

The sheep tipped its head to one side. *Really? Because there are thoughts bursting out of you. Going out on a lamb, I'd say you need help.*

If he'd been in human form he'd have laughed – sarcastically. Hares had the wrong mouth shape for laughing. But if he was in human form, he wouldn't be having this conversation. Human ears weren't built to understand animal speech. He sat back on his tail. *You want to help me? You do know you're only a sheep, right?*

The sheep glanced down at itself. *I could be some other four-legged woolly animal that says 'baaaa'. You never know.*

Two other sheep ambled closer and the three of them stood in a semi-circle, watching with polite interest. The hare shrugged. *All right, what do you want?*

Want? the first sheep asked. *We're sheep, why should we want anything?*

We watch, the second one said. *We notice. We observe.*

The third sheep nudged the hare with her head. *It's interesting, watching the world turn. You should try it.*

He didn't have time to just watch. Either the professors would find Storm or his aunt would, and either way the result would be the same. Storm wasn't safe here, but where else could he go?

David wriggled his nose and changed into a boy. He did it a bit too fast and it hurt.

'Ouch,' he said, stretching his arms until his elbows cracked.

The sheep stood around him. Not surprised at his sudden change, just observing.

David sighed and tore up a handful of grass, letting the blades scatter one at a time. Maybe he should just stay out of all this. He'd be moving on soon, anyway. None of it would matter then.

But he couldn't, of course. If he did nothing, either the professors or Ceridwen would come for Storm, and Jessie would be in greater danger than she could ever imagine.

A cold wind blew across the hillside, bringing a scattering of rain. A storm was coming – tomorrow at four o'clock, according to the professors' map.

David scrambled up. Storm was outside Odin's protection here in the mortal world, Ceridwen had said. The answer was obvious, then – Storm had to leave the mortal world. Then the professors could waste all the time they wanted looking for him; Ceridwen too. Jessie would be safe, and even though she'd have to lose Storm he'd still be alive.

Just for a moment, sunlight flooded the hillside.

'Thanks, sheep!' David shouted.

A chorus of *baaa*s followed him as he raced to the road. First, he'd cast protection spells around Jessie's house. That'd stop the professors finding Storm. And then, because he couldn't tell Jessie the truth, he'd have to talk to Storm.

CHAPTER 26

It was nearly eight o'clock in the morning on Friday, the seventh of September, and Abergavenny was quiet, apart from the occasional jogger, a few early dog walkers and three men in a silver car.

'Excuse me,' Professor Utterby said, leaning out of the car window to accost a lady with a black Labrador on a lead. 'Is that your dog?'

The Labrador cowered away from the car.

The lady frowned. 'Yes, she's mine. What has she done?'

Professor Utterby threw a handful of green powder into her face. 'Nothing. Please forget you saw us.'

A little over a minute later, the lady jumped, stared down at the empty lead and let out a cry. 'Sooty! Where's my Sooty?'

'Excuse me,' said Professor Nuffield, walking up to a group of three men a little later on. 'Is that your dog?'

The three men swung round together. None of them looked like the kind of person Professor

Nuffield cared to talk to. He took a spray bottle out of his pocket and squirted the air. The men froze. So did the dog, unfortunately, and Professor Nuffield had to pick it up and sprint, puffing, back to the car.

Professor Ryston had given up looking for stormhounds and was on his way back to the school to meet the others. He hoped they'd had better luck. Professor Utterby had been in such a bad mood this morning that Ryston had left the hotel early to go for a walk, just to get away from the shouting.

He kept his divining rods out, more from habit than because he really expected to find anything. They'd searched this whole town six times over now, taken every dog they'd come across and questioned them, and found nothing. It was as if the stormhound had disappeared into thin air.

One of the divining rods jumped in Ryston's hand. He paused, and looked at the entirely ordinary row of terraced houses. *Nothing to see here.*

The second rod turned full circle, then pointed up at the sky. The other one dipped sharply, straight towards the pavement. Ryston gave them both a shake and steadied them.

That house at the end of the row. It looked exactly the same as all the others – even more ordinary, if that were possible – but every time he tried to point his divining rods at it, they jerked away, almost as if something was batting them aside.

A tabby cat hissed at him from the wall in front of the last but one house.

'You can go away,' Ryston told it. It was fairly safe to assume that a cat was not going to turn out to be a stormhound in disguise.

On the other hand, cats noticed things, and there was definitely something strange going on here. It was worth a try, Ryston thought, pushing his useless divining rods into his pockets and grabbing the animal.

He realized his mistake seconds later when the cat turned on him and he found himself clutching a writhing, howling bundle of tabby fur, full of claws and teeth. Ryston dropped her, and she took off down the road. He paused to wipe blood from several deep scratches on his hands, and set off in pursuit.

Ryston cornered the cat under a bush some time later and threw a handful of Professor Utterby's sleeping powder at her.

'My apologies, cat,' he said, wrapping her in his coat. 'But my friends and I would like a word with you.'

CHAPTER 27

Jessie woke to a sharp howl that sounded like a cat, but when she looked out of the window she couldn't see anything. She lay back down for a minute, replaying her latest dream in her head. It had been the most vivid one yet. Racing through the sky with mountains far below and houses nestled between them . . .

. . . and dogs and horses all around her, thunder and lightning crashing, and a sense of wild freedom that made her bedroom feel like a prison.

And she remembered the man. He'd ridden a grey horse at the front of the pack. His helmet had been bronze with silver horns, his grey hair flowing out beneath it. At one point he'd turned and looked straight at Jessie and, even though it was only a dream, she'd gasped, because where his right eye should be, there was nothing but a long scar, cutting diagonally across his face.

Jessie reached for her sketchpad. She'd unknowingly filled another two pages with sharp, angry lines. Although they didn't seem to form any proper picture, they gave her the same sense of freedom she'd felt in the dream. Then she turned the page and froze, staring, because there was the face from the dream, sketched in grey pencil. Jessie's skin prickled. She could just about imagine scribbling lines in her sleep, but drawing an entire portrait – how had she managed that?

And why did the face look so familiar all of a sudden?

She grabbed her pencil and started adding lines to the face, turning the man's frown into a smile. That looked better. She drew in a horse behind him, and the outline of other riders in similar armour. Her pencil flew across the page so fast it felt like she was remembering this scene and not inventing it.

Storm scrabbled at her door.

Jessie fumbled for her phone and, forgetting the drawing, sat up straight in a panic when she saw it was past eight o'clock.

There was no time to take Storm for a walk this morning. Jessie opened the back door for him and he shot out into the garden with an excited yap. She stepped out after him. The weather seemed to be all things at once: the sun was bright, but there was a sharp wind and that slight prickling in the air that meant rain wasn't far away.

Four o'clock, Friday the seventh, she thought, remembering the map in the professors' staffroom.

It was Friday the seventh now. What was going to happen at four o'clock? She'd have to ask David again – but then she remembered David was no longer her friend, and she clenched her fists hard, wanting to shout out in frustration.

'Dad said he has to go to work early today,' Ben said, coming outside. 'He said I can come home for lunch today.' He kicked at the ground. 'Do we have to go to school?'

Jessie heaved a sigh. 'I'm afraid so. It'll be better today, you'll see. If any of the kids bother you, you should tell a teacher.'

'I'll just tell them I'm going to live with Mum in the holidays,' Ben said.

Jessie hugged him quickly. Then she noticed Mrs Williams staring at them from next door and she tensed, ready to be shouted at.

'I can't find Nutmeg,' Mrs Williams said. 'She always comes home for breakfast. 'Your dog better not have scared her.'

Storm raised his head and barked sharply.

'We've only just come out here,' Ben said indignantly.

Mrs Williams sniffed disbelievingly, but she looked more worried than angry.

'I heard a cat outside a little while ago,' Jessie said. 'It might have been Nutmeg.' She picked Storm up. 'Sorry, we've got to go to school. We'll help you look for Nutmeg when we get back if you like.'

'I can make posters,' Ben offered. 'Jessie can draw a picture of Nutmeg if you don't have any photos. She's good at drawing.'

Mrs Williams softened a little. 'Yes, well, I expect Nutmeg will be back by then. You should keep an eye on your dog too. My niece said her neighbour's dog disappeared for hours yesterday and looked really peculiar afterwards.'

'We'll be careful,' Jessie promised.

First Viking, now Nutmeg. Jessie took Storm inside and shut him in the back room. 'Please stay there today,' she said. She didn't like to leave him alone, but he'd be safe in the house. And, while Storm was safely asleep, she was going to find out the truth.

But not with David this time. Jessie slammed her sketchbook into her school bag. She didn't need David to work this out. He was part of the mystery anyway – he and his aunt, the professors, Jessie's dreams, all felt like part of the same puzzle. She knew David would never tell her the truth, and that only left her one option: the professors.

CHAPTER 28

Storm waited while the humans fussed about and left for school and work. Finally, when the house was quiet, he lay down, letting his ears flop over his eyes. He must have eaten too many meaty chunks because he felt queasy. All might be quiet now, but he'd heard a cat howling just before Jessie woke up, and the sound of footsteps. It had to be the professors. They were looking for him, and if they'd taken the cat they must be drawing closer.

Also, if they'd taken the cat, then the cat was in trouble. Storm jumped, trying to reach the key, but even though he caught it in his teeth he couldn't turn it. He paused, panting.

And then he barked in surprise because a white hare suddenly appeared in a shower of earth by the fence.

Storm got to his feet, growling softly. The hare hopped closer, right up to the back door. It might be a hare now, but Storm recognized the stink of Not-Boy even through the glass.

What are you doing here? Storm growled. *Begone!*

Or what? You'll chase me all over the garden? Tear me limb from limb? I don't think so. I'm not afraid of you.

Storm sniffed. *Yes you are. I can smell it.*

The hare hopped back a step. *Yes, all right*, it agreed, *I am a bit afraid of you. My aunt says you're a slavering monster who will kill everyone in the town.*

Storm didn't even know what 'slavering' meant. *Your aunt is deranged. If I'm so dangerous, why are you here? Why aren't you fleeing in terror?*

Because I want to talk to you. The hare's ears quivered. *And there's a door between us. That should stop you if you get any ideas.*

Yes, the annoying door. Storm headbutted the glass. *Turn into a boy and open it for me. I won't bite you.*

I know you won't, said the hare, *because I'm not going to do it. For a start, I don't have a key. I could try an opening charm, but my aunt doesn't like me casting spells. And if I turned into a boy we wouldn't be able to talk.*

I don't see why that matters. Open the door.

Tell me why you want to get out so badly?

Storm's fur prickled in annoyance. *The cat from next door did me a favour and now she has disappeared. She is irritating, but she's old. Also, she's a cat, so she isn't very intelligent. She may be in trouble and require rescue.*

The hare didn't respond for a moment, then it cocked its head to one side, blinking slowly. *I'm sorry. Did you just say you wanted to rescue a cat? You're a strange sort of stormhound.*

Storm bared his teeth. *What do you know of stormhounds? The cat acted in my service so I have a duty to her. Besides, if anything happens to her, the Valkyrie-Lady next door will blame Jessie, and . . . and if Jessie is upset she will not serve me so well,* he finished, slightly unconvincingly. He didn't like the thought of Jessie being upset.

The hair wriggled its nose. *The thing is I can't risk letting you out. The professors are hunting you and they're growing more desperate. If they have the cat and you go running to the rescue, they'll catch you and that'll be the end of you.*

I am not afraid, Storm said.

I know you're not. You're a dog, and dogs are too stupid to be afraid.

Now that was stepping over impudence into insult. If the door hadn't been in the way, Storm would have taught the hare a lesson. But it *was* in the way and no amount of jumping at it helped.

The hare watched him until he gave up, panting.

Calm down, will you? it said. *Tell you what. You stay here, and I'll rescue the cat. I know where*

the professors are staying.

Storm's backside hit the mat in surprise. *You? Why would you do that, Not-Boy?*

Because I'm Jessie's friend too, the hare said. It paused to scratch. *And, also, because you're going to make me a promise. If I save the cat, you have to leave. There's a storm brewing. I don't know if the Wild Hunt are looking for you, but if they are today is your best chance. Go back to the place where you fell, and do whatever you need to do to call them to you. You'll leave this world and you won't return – ever.*

That should be the easiest bargain in the world to make. Storm wanted to go back. That was the whole point of waiting here, why he'd put up with the indignities he'd suffered every day at the hands of the humans who knew no better. Because he knew it wouldn't be long until the Hunt returned.

Why then was he suddenly hesitating? *Maybe I wish to stay*, he said. Where had those words come from? Of course he didn't wish to stay.

The hare blinked several times and shook its head. *You know people are hunting you? The three professors, and my aunt too. What if they find you when Jessie is here? What do you think she will do?*

She'd try to protect him, like she had at the obedience class, not knowing the danger she was in. *I will defend her*, Storm barked, pawing at the locked door.

You? You can't even leave the house on your own. Take a good look at yourself, stormhound. Whatever you are in your world, you're nothing but a puppy here.

Storm looked at his reflection in the door. A puppy. Not a stormhound. Not important, not magnificent or fierce. And he knew the hare was telling the truth: if the hunters found him here and Jessie fought them, she'd lose. Her little spark of magic was no match for them.

I'm trying to protect her too, the hare said. *Believe it or not, she was my friend. This really is the only way she can be safe. Please.*

Storm turned to look behind him at the familiar kitchen with its cupboards and boxes, and the hall where he'd left scratch marks. Maybe Jessie would choose a new dog when he left: the white terrier she'd always wanted, or one of the others in the dog prison. He imagined another dog comforting her as she lay on her bed, another dog going out with her for walks, and it felt that the empty space inside him had spread to consume him.

But he was a stormhound, and he belonged to the Wild Hunt, not to this world with all its confusion. Storm bowed his head. *Very well. You have my word as a stormhound.*

The hare lowered its head too. Maybe it understood what it had cost Storm to promise this. *Don't feel bad*

about this, it said. *My aunt says there's a right place for everything, and everything should stay there. We'll be moving on soon as well. I've put a protection around this house so you'll be safe until I get back.*

Wait, Storm barked, but the hare was gone in a flash of white fur.

CHAPTER 29

It's not a good idea to lock a cat in a hotel room – especially if the cat doesn't want to be there. The moment the animal had woken, she'd knocked over all the candles. Then she'd run around in a panic and torn holes in Professor Utterby's best pyjamas, and now she was in the process of destroying the armchair. And the *noise* – Professor Utterby had heard the cries of demons rising from the Otherworld, and even that didn't compare to the wails and shrieks that filled the air now. It was a good job he'd cast a soundproof charm on the room or they'd have the hotel manager banging on the door asking what they were doing.

'It's no use carrying on like that,' he said, frowning as the cat tore a lump of pink cloth off the chair. 'No one can hear you.'

Normally, he liked cats. They knew they were a superior species and they weren't afraid to show it, but this was becoming tiresome. Time was pressing on – they had a matter of hours to find the stormhound and they were close, he could sense it.

'I'm not sure the cat knows anything,' Professor Nuffield said. He had a large claw mark across his nose.

Ryston was in even worse shape, with holes in his jumper and several deep scratches on his hands. 'I'm supposed to be teaching art today,' he complained. 'If I'd known the cat would be this much trouble I wouldn't have bothered taking it. Can't we just let it go?'

'In a minute.' Utterby picked up one of the fallen candles and relit it. The smoke smelled vaguely fishy with a hint of wet earth. The cat stopped yowling and hissed, its green eyes narrowing to horizontal slits. Professor Utterby held a finger in the candle flame. It was pleasantly cool and tickled a little. 'Mistress cat,' he said politely, 'we meant you no harm.' His voice translated into a series of mews and hisses. 'We simply wish to converse and then you'll be free to go.'

Converse with your own species, the cat hissed. *I am the cat who walks alone . . .*

'Why does every cat say that?' Nuffield sighed.

Utterby glared at them both. 'I am trying to do serious magic here. Go and wait outside if you can't be quiet.' He turned back to the cat. 'There is magic afoot,' he said. 'A creature of the Otherworld is here in Abergavenny, a stormhound of the Wild Hunt. We believe you may know something about it.'

Candle smoke coiled through the room. The cat

stared at him with wide, dilated pupils. Everything was quiet except for the sound of Ryston's coughing and the scrape of the window as he opened it a crack.

Utterby sat down on the wrecked armchair. 'Now,' he said, 'have you seen the stormhound?'

The cat appeared to be trying to bite its own tongue in the effort of not speaking. Utterby lit a second candle and more smoke drifted across the room.

I have seen it, the cat hissed, its tail switching back and forth. The words were dragged out one at a time. *Black . . . small . . .*

Professor Utterby leaned closer. 'Where? Where is the stormhound?'

He was interrupted by a sudden knocking on the door.

'Professor Utterby? Are you there? I've had a report about a cat.'

Professor Utterby stood back with a sigh of irritation. 'Did someone happen to let the manager see what we were doing?'

'It's not my fault,' Ryston said at once.

The manager knocked on the door again, louder this time. 'Professor Utterby?' The handle jiggled.

Professor Utterby opened the door a crack. 'I was sleeping. What's this about a cat?'

At the same moment, the window on the far side of the room shot up. Professor Utterby swung round, but the cat was faster. She darted across the room, clawed her way up Ryston's legs and was gone.

Utterby ran to the window. 'Ryston, you buffoon!'

'I didn't do anything,' Ryston protested.

Was that a flash of a white tail, disappearing into the bushes?

Utterby slammed the window shut in frustration.

'There's no cat?' asked the manager. 'Because if there is it'll cost extra.'

'No,' Utterby said tightly. 'There is no cat. Good day.'

He shut the door and turned back to his colleagues. *Black, small.* Where had he seen a small, black dog?

Of course! The obedience class with that irritating woman who also ran the Dog Rescue Centre. Now he thought about it, he remembered a black puppy growling at him, and a girl. He couldn't for the life of him remember her name or exactly what she looked like, which was odd because he was sure he'd seen her at school.

'You two pack up here, then go back to the house where Ryston found the cat, and keep watch,' he said. 'Take the car, and for goodness' sake don't let anyone see you. I will meet you shortly.' He looked out of the window at the gathering clouds, and smiled. The girl clearly had some magical protection of her own, and they wanted to recruit new students, didn't they? This could work out very well indeed.

CHAPTER 30

David wasn't in school that morning and when Jessie went looking for the professors at morning break she found their staffroom locked and no amount of jiggling the door handle would open it.

'I'm having a birthday party next Friday,' Prisha said as they were making their way down the stairs at lunchtime. 'Do you want to come?'

The question took Jessie by surprise. Why not? A party would be fun – something normal after all this week's weirdness.

'I'll have to check with Dad,' Jessie said. 'But thanks, I'd like that.'

They passed the corridor that led to the professors' staffroom and Jessie paused.

'Are you coming for lunch?' Prisha asked.

'No, I need to go home to check on my dog.' Jessie felt the corner of her sketchbook as she shifted her bag on her shoulder. 'I'll see you later.'

She waited until Prisha was out of sight, then, her heart thumping, she turned and ran back down the corridor. *One more try, just in case.*

She listened at the door then knocked gently and tried the handle.

The door jerked open so suddenly that she jumped.

Professor Utterby frowned out at her. Behind him, Jessie could see that the room was a mess, books and candles scattered everywhere. Professors Ryston and Nuffield were nowhere to be seen. At least she didn't have to face all three of them together, but Professor Utterby seemed somehow sterner and more frightening without the other two.

'My name is Jessie Price,' she said, shifting her bag from one shoulder to the other. 'I wondered, I mean, I thought . . .'

'You thought you'd pay me a visit.' Professor Utterby beamed at her. 'This is a coincidence. I was looking for you.'

'You were?' Jessie edged back a step. 'Who are you? I know you're not from Bangor University.'

'What makes you think that?' Professor Utterby asked her. 'Did you divine it?'

'No, I looked up the university website.'

Professor Utterby sighed. 'Young people nowadays . . . Nothing is secret. I *am* a professor, but not of any university you'll have heard of – and not of any subject you'll have heard of, either.' He opened the door wider. 'But I'm being most rude keeping you in the corridor. Come inside and we can discuss this properly.'

Jessie shook her head. 'No thanks.' She pulled her sketchbook out of her bag and turned to the drawing of the one-eyed man. 'I just wanted to ask you about this. Do you know who it is?'

Professor Utterby took the book off her. 'This is quite an extraordinary likeness. When did you meet Odin of the Wild Hunt?'

Jessie swayed, the smell from the candle in the room making her dizzy. 'I dreamed it. The Wild Hunt is just a legend – Professor Nuffield said so.'

Professor Utterby shrugged. 'Myths, legends, stories. They are all words for facts that people have forgotten.' He snapped her book shut and held it out to her, stepping back so she had to walk into the staffroom to take it.

Professor Utterby picked a petal out of a bowl and dropped it into the candle flame. Instead of shrivelling, it lay there, dipping up and down gently in the warmth.

Jessie stared.

'Elemental magic,' Professor Utterby said. 'As I was saying, I am no ordinary professor. I am one of the last three members of an institution known as the Invisible College, an institution established in the sixteenth century and devoted wholly to the research of the forbidden arts.'

The petal exploded in the candle flame with a little pop and a flare of purple light.

Jessie clutched her sketchbook like a shield. 'You're magicians?' This had to be a joke. Magic didn't exist. But then she remembered Professor Utterby's chemistry class, and Professor Nuffield talking about myths as if he believed them. And David and his aunt – if they were investigating the professors, did they know about this? Were they magicians too?

Professor Utterby put a hand on her shoulder, stopping her from backing away. 'You might not realize this, but you have potential in the dark arts. You've been defending yourself against my spells without even knowing it. Nuffield, Ryston and myself use the magic of this world, what little there is of it, but you have a rare and precious gift. You seem to attract the magic of the Otherworld, just like a tree attracts lightning. Your dreams are full of the Wild Hunt, you disrupt our magic,' he added, 'and, of course, you have a stormhound as a pet.'

The candles smoked, turning the air into a blur. Jessie's cheeks burned. He was talking about Storm, but Storm was just a puppy.

'I should have worked it out sooner,' Professor Utterby said. 'But I never imagined the Hounds of Annwn started off as puppies and grew.' His hand, resting on Jessie's shoulder, seemed to pin her to the floor so she couldn't move. 'I had the same hunger for knowledge when I was your age,' he said. 'I wanted to know everything and I didn't care what it cost me.

But you will have teachers – three of us. And we'll be recruiting other students as well, of course, so you won't be on your own. You'll be part of a tradition that goes back centuries. All you have to do is give me your dog.'

Storm. Jessie shook her head slowly. A Hound of Annwn. A stormhound from her dreams.

'All learning must begin with sacrifice,' Professor Utterby said. 'It will be worth it, I promise. Otherworld magic is vastly more powerful than anything this world has to offer.'

Jessie stared at him in disbelief. 'You're mad. Magic isn't . . .'

'Isn't real?' Professor Utterby asked with a smile. 'You know better than that. You've felt it, I'm sure. There are bigger things in this world, things that cannot be explained.'

No – he had to be wrong. And yet something in his words felt right. It was like that picture in the Dog Rescue Centre, random dots that suddenly became a castle and you knew it was there all along, you just hadn't seen it because you weren't looking properly.

'It's a lot to take in, isn't it?' Professor Utterby asked. 'But you don't have to learn everything at once. All we need for now is the dog.'

His words jolted Jessie back to reality – a bigger, stranger reality, but some things hadn't changed. Professor Utterby didn't know anything if he thought she'd hand Storm over to him. She relaxed and started to nod. Then, as Professor Utterby smiled back and released his grip on her, she twisted away and ran for the door.

'Stop!' Professor Utterby cried, as fresh air flooded in on her.

Jessie kept running. She skidded round the corner and bumped into Mr Heron who was coming the other way. 'Sorry!' she shouted.

'Ah, Professor Utterby,' she heard Mr Heron say. 'May I have a quick word?'

Jessie ran out into the playground with a sob of relief. She'd be in trouble for skipping school, but that was the least of her worries. She had to reach Storm before the professors found him. She sprinted across the grey playground and into the street as rain started to fall.

CHAPTER 31

Storm sat inside the back door of the house and watched, helpless as a cat – no, even worse than that, because a cat could probably find a window to climb through and escape. Helpless as a sheep, more like. Storm rubbed at the smears his nose had made on the door.

He should never have trusted the Not-Boy. That was where he'd gone wrong – handing a rescue mission over to someone else. Now Storm had no idea what was going on and was imagining all sorts of things. What if the professors had captured the Not-Boy? What if he'd told them about Jessie? They could be on their way here this very moment.

The front door opened. Storm sprang up, barking. *You'd better not be the professors!*

Jessie's Dad came into the kitchen. Storm let his tail drop down.

'Hello, Storm,' Jessie's Dad said, sounding tired.

Storm ran to him and pawed his trousers gently. *Jessie's Dad, I require you to open the back door*

so I may go into the garden.

Jessie's Dad frowned and pushed him off gently. 'Sorry, Storm, not now. It's just started to rain, and I have to tidy up.'

Storm didn't see what those two things had to do with each other. He watched Jessie's Dad pick up towels and fold them, and an idea formed. If Jessie's Dad wanted to tidy up so much, it would only be polite to help him. He scrambled up one of the kitchen chairs, being careful to leave claw marks in the seat, then he hopped on to the table and wagged his tail. Spoons and cups went flying.

'Storm, down,' Jessie's Dad said, running to rescue them. Storm wagged his tail harder.

I don't know what you're saying. I'm just an innocent puppy who wants to play. Preferably outside. He batted the final spoon off the table. It made a satisfying clang when it hit the floor.

Tell you what, you open the door for me and I'll leave your house alone. It's not raining that hard outside. Anyway, I'm a stormhound and I like bad weather.

Jessie's Dad picked him up and placed him gently but firmly on the floor. 'Stay, Storm.'

What? Right here? Hey, maybe I need the toilet now. Storm lifted his back leg and stared at Jessie's Dad threateningly.

Jessie's Dad groaned. 'All right. Just for a minute.

I don't want you getting all wet.'

He went to the door and turned the key in the lock. At last! Storm jumped impatiently.

But, before Jessie's Dad could open the door, a shrill ring came from the front door and he groaned even louder.

'She's early,' he said. 'Stay here, Storm.'

Stay? When someone was at their front door. It wouldn't be Jessie or Ben, because they'd let themselves in. Was it the Not-Boy, then? Or, worse, the professors?

Storm followed Jessie's Dad into the hall, tensed and ready to fight any intruders.

But it wasn't the Not-Boy or the professors. A lady stood on the doorstep, damp from the rain, her clothes smelling of car fumes.

'Hello, Stephen,' she said.

Storm froze where he was. He recognized that voice – he'd heard it come out of the telephone many times. It was the Mum-Person! He flattened himself to the floor, his tail thumping a warning. She was the one who'd made Jessie cry.

She's trouble. Don't let her in.

Jessie's Dad ignored him, and now the Mum-Person was stepping inside the house, putting down a bag and an umbrella. 'I'm sorry to spring this on you,' she said.

'It's fine.' Jessie's Dad didn't sound like it was fine.

He straightened a picture on the wall, then started picking up stray shoes. What did he want shoes for? Was he going out? No . . . Now he was putting the shoes in a tidy line. 'Jessie and Ben aren't back yet,' he said. 'Did you want a cup of tea or something?'

He was being terribly polite. This was why he'd wanted to clean up: because he knew the Mum-Person was coming. For some reason it was important for her to think their house was tidy.

'Did you tell them I was coming?' the Mum-Person asked. 'It's just that Jessie sounded so upset on the phone yesterday I couldn't stop worrying.'

And whose fault was that? Storm growled.

Jessie's Dad picked him up. 'I thought you could surprise them,' he said.

He didn't mean that. His scent always sharpened when he was lying. Storm didn't know why he'd lie, or why he wanted Jessie and Ben to be surprised.

'Actually,' Jessie's Dad said, 'I didn't want them being disappointed if you couldn't make it after all. They're both coming home for lunch today. Go into the front room – it's tidiest there. I'll just let Storm into the garden for a bit.'

He seemed to relax a little after that speech, as if the words had got bundled up inside him like a hairball, and he'd had to get them out.

'Thank you.' The Mum-Person dabbed at her eyes. 'I'm afraid I might be starting to react already.'

Storm squirmed in Jessie's Dad's arms. He didn't want to go out any more. He had to stay here to defend Jessie when she came home.

I am Storm of Odin and I will not be manhandled.

But apparently he would be. Jessie's Dad tucked him firmly under one arm and took him to the back door. 'There you go,' he said. 'You run around for a while, there's a good dog.'

The door closed, shutting him off from the Mum-Person. Storm scratched the door. *I've changed my mind. Let me back in. I'm sorry I messed up your kitchen, but you wouldn't listen.*

It was no use: the door remained shut. Storm lay against it with a sigh.

A few minutes later, a flash of tabby tore across the garden.

Storm leaped to his feet, his tail wagging. *Cat! You're back. Not that I care*, he added quickly, remembering himself. *What happened?*

The cat shuddered, her hair standing on end. *Dark magic. Magic that even a cat could not fight. Beware, stormhound, the hunters know what you are. They are coming for you.*

The Valkyrie-Lady from next door must have been watching because she came running outside. 'Nutmeg, where have you been?' She scooped the cat up. 'Naughty dog. Leave my cat alone.'

I wasn't touching your cat.

The Valkyrie-Lady threw a slipper at him, then turned and stamped back indoors, taking the cat with her. Storm nosed at the slipper. How many of these things did she have? Did she keep spare ones just for throwing? He sighed, then sneezed. At least he knew the cat was safe, but that meant he had a promise to keep.

The rain grew heavier. Storm padded to the tree and sat down under the shelter of its branches. He considered chewing up the Valkyrie-Lady's slipper, but he couldn't be bothered. What was the point of destroying one slipper if Odin laid waste to the whole town?

The space inside him felt as vast as the sky, and the call of the Hunt echoed through it. He stood up. He was a stormhound, not a puppy. It was time he acted like one.

He walked to the fence and examined the ground. The earth was loose near the corner – it must have been where the hare had got in. Storm dug at it, scrabbling until he'd made a space the size of a puppy. Then he started to heave himself through. He'd grown in the past couple of weeks. He had to drag himself, panting hard. His collar caught on a jutting edge of wood and started to tear. But eventually it was done. He stood on the other side, panting and shaking mud from his coat, his collar hanging half off.

He hadn't said goodbye, but maybe it was for the

best. Goodbyes made humans sad and he didn't want his last memory of Jessie to be a sad one. He started off down the road. If he could make it back to the mountains, he could find somewhere to hide. And then, if – no, *when* – the Hunt returned, he would . . .

He didn't even notice the tall woman, not until she stopped, shot out her hand and grabbed him by the scruff of his neck.

'I recognize you,' she said. 'Stormhound.'

CHAPTER 32

Storm shrank back on the pavement. The Not-Boy's aunt crouched in front of him, one hand pressing down on the back of his neck so he couldn't move. She smelled of fire and ancient woods. Old magic. Storm flattened himself to the ground, suddenly feeling how small he was in this body, how easy it would be for the woman to pick him up and walk off with him.

Ceridwen drew back a fraction, her scent becoming less ancient magic and more growing confusion. Rain fell around them in a steady rhythm.

'You're not exactly what I expected,' Ceridwen said.

Storm snapped at her, trying to twist out of her grip, cursing his silly puppy body that was too small, too weak to do anything.

'I can understand why Morfran tried to hide you, you looking like this,' Ceridwen said. 'Are you really a puppy? If this is a disguise, it is certainly convincing.' She lifted him up in one hand. 'I'm afraid you'll have to come with me.'

She didn't sound afraid. She sounded . . . sorry.

And then another voice. 'Stop!'

The Not-Boy. He came racing along the road, out of breath, his clothes flapping wetly.

'Auntie Ceridwen, wait!'

Ceridwen's fingernails dug into Storm's neck. He wriggled harder. *Unhand me. Ouch!*

Ceridwen ignored him. 'Did you think I wouldn't notice, Morfran? You come home late, you make friends with humans. And then I found your clumsy protection spells. I knew you were hiding something.'

The Not-Boy really *had* been trying to protect him.

Odin will reward you for this, Storm promised.

A car swished by on the road. Ceridwen shifted her grip on Storm, tucking him under one arm and keeping the grip on his neck with her other hand. 'I told you stormhounds are dangerous. You never listen, do you?'

'You're the one who doesn't listen!' The Not-Boy shouted. 'I was taking him back to the Hunt. He's only a puppy.'

Ceridwen held Storm up to look at him, as if checking how big he was.

He wagged his tail uncertainly. *See? Puppy. You can let me go, and I'll be on my way. I'll ask Odin to strike you with thundery vengeance another day.*

Ceridwen half smiled. 'I can understand you, you know, little stormhound.'

She wasn't sure what to do now. She didn't know

what to make of him. Storm wriggled.

But then her grip tightened on him again. 'Puppy or not, we can't have him running free in this world.'

'Why not?' the Not-Boy's face turned red. 'You keep saying that the worlds shouldn't mix, but you use magic all the time.'

'That's different.'

'How is it? You taught me how to use magic too. You taught me how to change shape, and now you want me to pretend I'm a boy. I'm not! If Storm shouldn't be here, then neither should I. Are you going to kill me too?'

Storm already knew the sorceress meant to harm him, so finding out she meant to kill him wasn't a surprise. It was surprising, however, how angry the Not-Boy sounded about it. He wriggled and managed to twist his body round a little until Ceridwen's fingers were across his nose. She let out a hiss of breath.

'Don't be ridiculous, Morfran.'

'I prefer the name David,' the Not-Boy said tightly. 'And I won't let you hurt Storm. He's harmless.'

Harmless? Speak for yourself, Not-Boy.

Storm growled, then he opened his mouth as wide as he could and sank his teeth into Ceridwen's hand. They were only puppy teeth, but they had the force of a desperate stormhound behind them. Ceridwen yelled, her grip loosening on him. Storm kicked her hard. His collar ripped away completely and the next moment he was falling.

He hit the pavement and ran.

'Storm!' the Not-Boy shouted.

Storm ran faster. A low roll of thunder shook the clouds overhead. His paws kicked up water as he raced through puddles. It was almost like being back in the Hunt, except he was on his own, and he was the prey this time, not one of the hunters.

He came to a road and dodged between cars. Horns sounded on either side of him. Glancing back, he saw the Not-Boy and his aunt, still holding the broken collar.

A silver car slowed.

Out of the way, Storm barked at it.

The back door opened and, too late, Storm saw the two eager faces inside. He tried to stop, to change direction, but he found himself lifted up and dragged backwards.

'Got him!' Professor Nuffield exclaimed.

CHAPTER 33

Jessie arrived back at the house, soaked and out of breath. 'Dad, Ben, I'm home. Where's Storm?'

She stopped, staring at the umbrella and the bag in the hall. Mum's umbrella. Mum's bag. Her heart leaped. It couldn't be – Mum was in London. This must be another trick of the professors.

But Ben shouted from the front room, 'Jessie, Mum's here!' And then, impossibly, Mum appeared in the doorway, her face breaking into a smile, her arms out.

'Hello, Lightning Bug,' she said. 'I've missed you.'

Jessie couldn't move, but it didn't matter because Mum was across the hall in two steps.

'Your hair's all wet,' she said. She pushed a strand of it off Jessie's face, then wrapped her arms round her.

'It's raining,' Jessie said, her voice muffled against Mum's shoulder. In that moment, Jessie didn't care about the professors, or David, or anything else at all. Mum was here, which meant that everything would be all right.

'It's just that you sounded so upset on the phone last night,' Mum said, drawing back. 'So I took the day off work and drove straight here. You don't mind, do you?'

Jessie wiped her eyes. 'Of course I don't mind. How long are you staying? The weekend?'

'If you'll let me. We can go shopping. And I've brought photos of the new flat. I thought you and Ben could choose the colours for your bedroom.'

'Red,' Ben said. 'I want it to be red – even the ceiling.'

'You can't have a red ceiling.' Jessie laughed.

'We can if we want. It's our room.'

Jessie's laughter caught in her throat. It wasn't 'their' room, though, was it? David had said that travelling between places meant you never belonged anywhere. But he was wrong – he had to be. They couldn't go through their lives not belonging.

Mum sneezed. 'Sorry – dog hair. I'll have to get used to that.'

'Storm's in the garden,' Dad said. 'He wanted to go out.'

Jessie stiffened, a sudden image of Professor Utterby flashing through her mind. She pushed past her mum and ran to the kitchen.

'We can paint the ceiling blue,' Ben shouted after her. 'Then we can lie in bed and pretend we're looking at the sky. And you can draw a picture of a castle for the wall.'

Ignoring him, Jessie flung open the back door. 'Storm! Come in – now.'

But the garden was empty.

No sign of Storm, not under the tree or in the flower bed. A single blue slipper lay on the grass. Jessie threw it back into next-door's garden and leaned over the fence to see if Storm had somehow got through. He wasn't there. She already knew he wouldn't be. A tight panic gripped her. Professor Utterby had said they wanted Storm, and now he was gone. They'd taken him, and she hadn't even noticed.

'I only let him out a few minutes ago,' Dad said. 'He must be here.' He bent down to look under the bushes in the flower bed.

Jessie stood shivering as Mum and Ben came outside too.

'It's the pet-nappers,' she said. Mum and Dad would never believe her if she told them the truth. 'They've been taking people's dogs and now they've got Storm.'

Dad hugged her. 'This is my fault. I shouldn't have let him out on his own. I thought he'd be all right in the garden. Don't worry – we'll find him. He can't have gone far.'

If the professors had taken Storm, he could be anywhere.

Jessie ran back to the house, grabbing her coat from the hall and squashing it on over her wet clothes. 'I'll go back towards school. You go and look around the castle – that's where we take him for walks. It'll be fine,' she said, seeing Ben's pale face. *Play along*, she thought, *pretend everything is all right, even when it isn't*.

She pulled Storm's lead from the hook in the kitchen and dashed out into the rain. If anyone had hurt Storm, she was going to make them very sorry.

She ran on. Then, halfway along the road that led to the school, she saw David and his aunt. They were standing by the traffic lights, arguing.

'David!' Jessie shouted.

They both turned – and as they did, Jessie saw something dangling from Ceridwen's hand: Storm's collar.

Jessie's stomach lurched. She sprinted up the last stretch of road, her feet pounding through puddles. 'What have you done with Storm?'

CHAPTER 34

Storm snapped at Professor Nuffield's hands. It did no good, but it was vaguely satisfying when Nuffield yelped in pain. Professor Utterby glanced back from the front seat. 'Will someone keep that dog under control?' he asked.

The two professors had first driven back to the school to collect Utterby. Now the car was moving out of town, taking Storm further away from safety, further away from Jessie.

He was a stormhound, Storm reminded himself, not a puppy. He was the one who'd chosen to leave Jessie and he didn't need the assistance of humans. In fact, he hoped Jessie didn't try to find him. He hoped he never saw her again – because, if she found him with the professors, there was no saying what they'd do to her. Knowing she was safe at home made Storm braver.

Professor Ryston sneezed, and dug a handkerchief out of his pocket. He wore a jumper that reminded Storm of the Fuzzy-Lady from the dog prison, except that Ryston's smelled of stale magic. Storm scrabbled across Nuffield's legs.

'Calm down, stormhound,' Professor Utterby said. 'We won't keep you long, and then you'll be free.'

Did they mean to send him back to the Hunt? Storm paused, but then Ryston sniggered. 'Free of life altogether,' he said.

That made Storm whine.

'Do you think he can understand us?' Nuffield asked.

Utterby braked sharply at a corner, jolting them all forward, then drove on. 'A creature of the Otherworld? I have no doubt of it.'

Maybe I'm not a creature of the Otherworld. Maybe I'm just an ordinary puppy and you're wasting your time.

'Some people say magic doesn't belong in this world,' Professor Utterby continued as if Storm hadn't said a word. It seemed they couldn't understand him. 'Can you believe that, stormhound? I believe magic should belong to everyone – anyone who wants it, that is. The Otherworld has hoarded it far too long.'

You just wait. I'll show you the power of the Otherworld, Storm growled. He felt his shadow begin to spread across the back seat.

'If you'd had to fight for every scrap of magic, you'd understand,' Professor Utterby said. 'We have devoted our lives to it, building on the traditions of those who came before us. Decades of study, of experimentation, of pushing the boundaries of knowledge. And then I found it – a few lines of a spell, at the back of an ancient book, the ink so faded we could barely read it.'

'I think this is the right dog, by the way,' Nuffield said, watching Storm's shadow writhe.

'Of course it is. A spell, stormhound, powerful enough to breach the barrier between our world and yours. It took a few attempts, but we did it – we reached into the Otherworld and brought a stormhound crashing down to earth.'

I don't care what you did. You will release me, or . . . Hold on, a spell?

Professor Nuffield wrapped the spare seat belt round him and pulled it tight, so Storm could barely move. He didn't resist. A strange lightness filled him. The professors had cast a spell. He hadn't fallen because he was too weak or too slow to keep up. It had been the professors' doing!

'I have to admit I was expecting something a bit more impressive than you,' Professor Utterby said. 'But you'll do. We know all about the power of stormhounds. Your blood, your hair, your tears. You are going to help us restore the Invisible College to its former glory. We can make a hundred different spells from your body. We will use them to seize yet more magic, we will reopen the college and train a whole new generation of sorcerers. We will tear such a rift in the barrier with the Otherworld that it will never close again.'

'I thought we were going to keep the stormhound's power for ourselves,' Professor Ryston said, coughing and shifting nervously away from Storm. 'I want a cure for asthma, remember.'

'There will be plenty of power to go round,' Utterby replied. 'We can afford to be generous.'

'But not too generous,' Nuffield said. He pulled stray wisps of hair out of his moustache. 'Maybe we could start with one student, someone to sweep the floors and wash the test tubes.'

'Or someone to answer the phones,' Ryston suggested wistfully. 'Like a real college.'

Silence settled like a weight. Abergavenny was far behind them, and the dark, broken shape of a mountain peak rose before them. Storm's ears pricked. He recognized that mountain – it was where he'd fallen into this world. He strained to see out of the car window. If he was right, the road would be bending round when it got to the hills, and he'd see trees, and . . .

A sheep wandered into the road, causing Professor Utterby to brake sharply. He sounded the horn, but the sheep didn't move. Another one meandered out into the road, followed by another, and another. Storm struggled against the seat belt. One of the sheep looked in through the side window at him.

Sheep, help! Storm barked.

Professor Utterby turned off the car engine. 'We have plenty of time. Let's not hurry and spoil things. Nuffield, keep hold of the dog. Ryston, go outside and move the sheep.'

'Why me?' Ryston grumbled.

'Because you're the youngest and you're supposed to do what your elders tell you. Jump to it.'

Professor Ryston muttered words that even Odin would have considered rude, and opened the car door to get out. Storm tried to dash after him, but the seat belt tangled round his body jerked him back. Ryston slammed the door again.

Storm lay panting slightly while Professor Nuffield hummed tunelessly, Professor Utterby drummed his fingers on the steering wheel and, outside, Professor Ryston chased sheep to and fro with his divining rods.

'If it's any consolation, young stormhound,' Professor Utterby said, watching his colleague. 'Your death will make a whole world of difference. To you as well, of course, but mainly to us.'

My death isn't going to happen.

Professor Utterby was taking Storm exactly where he needed to go. All he had to do was escape once they reached the mountain and wait for the Hunt to come.

As if in reply, a low growl of thunder ruffled the clouds. Outside, Ryston pointed his divining rods at the sheep and sparks flew out. The sheep bleated in alarm and scattered.

Storm flopped down on the seat, looking as if he'd given up, as Ryston climbed back in, dripping wet.

'We'll have to walk the last part so you'd have got wet anyway,' Professor Utterby said unsympathetically.

He started the car again. Storm's stomach lurched with the motion and with a strange mixture of hope and dread. If the Hunt didn't come in time, this could end badly. Never before had Storm feared he might die. It should have squashed him, but, oddly, it made him feel bigger, more alive. Was this what it felt like to be mortal?

CHAPTER 35

Jessie charged through the rain with a bellow she barely recognized as her own.

'Jessie, calm down,' David said.

'Calm down?' She made a grab for Storm's collar. 'That's Storm's. What have you done with him?'

David shook his head, his mouth half open as if he were trying to decide what to say – what lies to tell next. His aunt stepped back. 'We do not have your dog,' she said in a commanding tone. 'You did not see us here. You will go back home and forget about this.'

Jessie's thoughts swam. She pushed Ceridwen's hand aside.

'You're wasting your time,' David said. 'I told you, magic doesn't work properly on her. We have to tell her the truth.'

Magic. Jessie snatched Storm's collar out of Ceridwen's hand. 'I already know the truth. You're Ceridwen, the enchantress from the legend.'

Ceridwen's mouth set in a tight line. 'Her descendant, actually. She should have been content with this world, but she wanted more. She wanted to know everything. In the end, she went too far. She created a potion that would grant the gift of all wisdom, and in doing so, she brought magic into the world, where it does not belong. Her descendants have been trying to undo her mistake ever since, to seek out magic and contain it.'

'So when you guessed the professors were evil magicians and we are the magic police, you're weren't far wrong,' David said. He looked down at his feet. 'Sorry. I tried to keep you out of this. Ceridwen isn't really my aunt. When she found me, she called me Morfran to keep the story alive, but I wanted a more normal name, so I chose David.'

'She found you?' Jessie echoed.

David looked up at her, his eyes shining in the rain. 'That's the other thing,' he said. 'I'm not human.'

He shimmered and vanished, and a large, white hare blinked up at Jessie from the pavement.

Jessie screamed.

'Morfran!' Ceridwen snapped.

'Told you,' David said, turning back into himself with a smug grin.

Jessie's legs wobbled, but she clutched Storm's collar, locked her knees and glared at the boy who wasn't a boy. 'Very impressive. Where's Storm?'

Ceridwen raised an eyebrow. 'You said she was different. I think you might be right.'

'Says the sorceress who travels around with a talking hare,' said Jessie. She felt like she was back in her dream, full of lightning, ready to ride through anything in her way. 'Storm is my dog. I don't care what else the professors say he is. He's *mine*. That means I'm responsible for him. Where is he?'

Ceridwen gazed back at her, her expression hard as stone. 'There are two worlds,' she said slowly. 'Our world and the Otherworld – the world of myth and stories and magic. Your dog came from the Otherworld. He must go back there.'

David grinned; Jessie didn't know why.

'Professor Utterby said the magic of the Otherworld was more powerful than anything,' she said. She jerked back from Ceridwen in sudden alarm. 'That's why they want Storm – they're going to take his magic.'

Ceridwen nodded, her face stern. 'Morfran foolishly thought he could send the hound back to the Hunt without telling me. The professors snatched him. I don't know where they are now, but they'll be taking him to Mount Skirrid.'

'Four o'clock,' Jessie said, remembering the maps she'd seen in the staffroom. 'I'm coming with you.' Ceridwen started to scowl, and Jessie clenched her fists. 'I'll walk if I have to.'

Ceridwen sighed, then handed Jessie Storm's collar. 'Even if we save your stormhound, he cannot stay with you. He belongs to the Wild Hunt. He must go back. Do you understand, child?'

A sharp pain filled Jessie's chest. To save Storm, only to lose him forever? She'd only had him two weeks; it shouldn't hurt this much. She drew in an unsteady breath and swallowed back her tears.

'I want him to be happy,' she said. 'He can't be properly happy here when he belongs somewhere else.'

Ceridwen gave her a look that was almost approving. 'He will be himself with the Hunt. You should always let people be who they really are.'

For a moment, her gaze strayed to David, then she frowned and turned away. 'They'll want to be on Skirrid's peak when the storm is overhead so we have a little time.'

Jessie followed her, wondering where she was going. 'Are you really a hare?' she whispered to David.

'Really.' He gave her a nervous grin. 'I was the last of my litter. A fox got the rest of them. Ceridwen found me and decided to keep me. She saved my life, basically.' The look he shot at his aunt's back was filled with pride. 'Of course, she's not really my aunt, but we feel like we're sort of family. She taught me how to transform and how to cast magic spells.'

'What's it like?' Jessie asked.

David shrugged. 'It's normal for me, so it's hard to tell. I prefer being a boy usually, and Auntie Ceridwen prefers it too. She likes everything to fit neatly into one place – and I think she was probably breaking a few rules when she saved me.'

Jessie looked at the tall figure striding in front. Ceridwen didn't look like the rule-breaking type.

'Why did she do it?'

'Because I felt like it,' Ceridwen snapped. 'Or would you prefer I travelled this world, keeping all of you safe, entirely on my own.' She walked to where her orange-and-black motorbike stood under a tree. 'Let's be clear,' she said. 'I'm not doing this for you. If it was up to me, I'd remove the stormhound from the mortal world the easy way. But, for some reason, Morfran seems to like you, so I'll make an exception. Once, and once only.' She handed Jessie a motorcycle helmet.

David grinned and bounced on his heels.

'Don't expect me to come running the next time you get into trouble,' Ceridwen told him. 'You'd better change. There's no room for the three of us as we are.'

David shimmered and changed. Though Jessie stared, she couldn't work out the exact moment when the boy became the hare. She tried to smile, but her face felt stiff with nerves. She took out her phone and sent a message to Dad: *With David and his aunt. They're helping look for Storm.*

Just in case something happened to her.

She put on her helmet and swung her leg over the bike behind Ceridwen. David hopped up between them and wedged himself in.

'Hold tight,' Ceridwen said as the bike sped off.

CHAPTER 36

The professors' car lurched to a stop at the side of a field. The sky was black with cloud by now, the air so thick with rain Storm couldn't see out of the front window. He tensed, digging his claws into the seat. Professor Ryston wheezed and puffed on one side of him, and Nuffield sat on the other, studying a map. Storm had taken a bite out of it, earning himself a whack across the nose, which he added to the list of indignities punishable by smiting. It was getting to be quite a long list.

But here they were – back where it had all started. Storm recognized the trees and the large sign on the other side of the road.

Professor Ryston got out of the car and hauled a large bag out of the back. He returned with a chain, which he fastened round Storm's neck. Storm had been prepared to run, but his legs suddenly felt as weak as clay. He tottered off the car seat and tumbled out into the rain.

'Mountain iron,' Professor Utterby said. 'Mined at

midnight, and containing enough magic to control even a full-grown stormhound, let alone a puppy like you. It should keep you quiet. Ryston, do you have the apparatus?'

Ryston shook the bag at him. Several items inside clinked. Storm saw the outline of something sharp through the material. A knife, maybe? He shuddered and staggered back to his feet, shaking rain from his coat. Even this effort left him breathless.

Utterby took hold of Storm's chain. 'Lead on, then, Nuffield.'

They set off across the field, Utterby keeping a tight grip on the chain and tugging on it every time Storm stumbled.

The hill grew steeper and the grass of the field gave way to trees. Sheep ambled around the trunks, not interfering as the three men and the dog climbed the slope, but keeping an eye on things.

Don't feel baaaaaaad, one of them bleated to Storm. *All's wool that ends wool.*

Professor Ryston tripped on a tree root.

'Be careful with the equipment, will you?' Professor Utterby snapped.

Ryston dumped the bag down. 'You carry it if you're that worried about it.'

The professors really didn't like each other: that was useful to know. Storm lay down, whining as if in pain.

'Nuffield, you take the dog. I'll carry the bag,' Professor Utterby muttered in annoyance.

Nuffield bent over Storm, intending to pick him up. Storm waited until he could see every yellow hair in the professor's moustache, then, with the last of his strength, he lunged. His teeth closed over the end of Nuffield's moustache. Nuffield gave a muffled yell of pain, staggered back and fell down on his bottom, letting go of the chain. Storm spat out a mouthful of moustache and scrabbled over the professor's head, tumbling back downhill. Ryston shouted and ran after him, but tripped over a sheep that suddenly appeared.

Run, storm puppy!

He was trying! But the chain had got itself wrapped round his middle and he felt like he was suffocating. Then Utterby jumped on top of him, squashing him flat.

'Can't we kill him now?' Ryston asked, wheezing.

Utterby stood up, holding Storm tight round the middle. Storm tried to kick him, but his legs wouldn't obey him. He sagged, his strength all gone. All he could do was hang there as Utterby carried him back up the mountain slope.

But then Storm heard a crashing of branches behind, too loud for any sheep, and then Jessie's voice, angry as the lightning, shouting his name.

Jessie! Storm barked. Jessie had come for him. Fear surged through him and, with it, a burst of new energy. He struggled wildly. Jessie should not have come. She was only human, only a child. She couldn't hope to fight the professors. But she'd come nevertheless.

'Storm!' she cried. She came striding through the trees like something out of the Wild Hunt – wet and furious. And she wasn't alone, Storm saw. The Not-Boy and his aunt were right behind her.

Storm kicked Utterby again and slithered out of his grip, landing upside down on the grass.

'That's my dog,' Jessie said. She picked up a tree branch and brandished it like a weapon. 'Give him back.'

Storm's heart almost burst with pride. He rolled over, trying to avoid the professors' hands as they grabbed at him. Professor Utterby straightened his coat. 'The dog does not belong to you, or to anybody else in this world. We have urgent need of its magic. I suggest the three of you leave now, before this turns nasty.'

Ceridwen began to laugh.

'I'm quite serious,' Utterby said. 'If you think we're giving you the dog just so you can kill it . . .'

'I have no intention of killing the dog,' Ceridwen said. 'Not any more. Morfran, Jessie, the first chance you get, take Storm and run. I'll follow you.' Rain sizzled around her, turning to steam. 'Gentlemen,' she continued, 'I am Ceridwen, Guardian of Knowledge in this world and, by all the laws of magic, I challenge you. You will hand over the stormhound and leave.'

Jessie lowered her tree branch, looking confused, but Storm knew exactly what had happened, and so did the Not-Boy, judging by his sudden yelp of dismay.

'A sorcerer's challenge,' the Not-Boy said. 'They have to accept or surrender, and they can't do anything else until they've chosen.' He looked at them hopefully. 'They might surrender, of course.'

'Can she do this?' Nuffield asked.

'Apparently so,' Professor Utterby said. He gestured, and a staff appeared in his hand. 'Gentlemen?'

Ryston put down his bag and took out his divining rods. They became a shield and sword. Nuffield was suddenly holding an axe.

No chance of surrender, then. Storm barked a warning to Jessie: *Stay out of this.*

But he knew she couldn't understand him, and he guessed that even if she could, she'd take no notice.

'Challenge accepted,' Professor Utterby said. A ball of light gathered around the tip of his staff.

'Earthfire,' Ceridwen scoffed. 'Is that the best you can do?'

Storm's fur crackled with energy. Ceridwen hissed and the chain round his neck became a snake. Professor Utterby found himself holding its tail and he dropped it with a yell.

Storm jumped back, a weight like a mountain

suddenly lifting from him so that, for a moment, he felt like he was flying.

'Run!' Ceridwen yelled. She raised her hands and the trees around flashed with silver light.

No! He was a stormhound. He didn't run away. He snapped at Professor Utterby's heels. *You want my magic? Come and take it!*

Professor Ryston banged his sword on his shield. The air seemed to contract for a moment, then a rush of wind ripped through the hillside. Storm felt himself being lifted half up. He dug his claws into the ground and tried to hang on, but the wind blew him sideways and he landed painfully. Leaves and branches flew past him and a terrified sheep ran away. Ceridwen gave a cry like a bird and became an eagle. She launched herself into the sky and circled higher, rising above the wind that fought to bring her down.

'Storm!' Jessie gasped as he flung himself at her. She scooped him up and for a second he almost forgot he was a stormhound. He licked her face frantically, feeling his tail wagging against her arms.

Then a scream broke the sky. The white eagle was plunging down, claws outstretched. Lightning cracked between the trees. A patch of grass caught fire and blazed briefly before the rain put it out. Ceridwen landed, transforming back into human form. But she stumbled, and Storm smelled magic bleeding out of her. She was burning through her power too quickly.

She shouldn't have challenged the professors. She could hold them off for a while, but she couldn't beat them.

She couldn't . . . but Odin could.

The thought cut through him, bright as lightning. Storm squirmed out of Jessie's arms and dashed away up the slope.

CHAPTER 37

One moment Jessie was clutching Storm tightly, the next he was dashing away through the trees.

'Storm, come back!' she shouted.

He turned his head and barked, then ran on. He wanted them to follow. David hung back and she caught his wrist and pulled him.

He shook his head. 'I'm not leaving Ceridwen.'

'You have to. She told us to run. Storm knows what he's doing.'

She glanced back to see Ceridwen throw Professor Ryston into a tree. The sorceress turned round. A trickle of blood snaked down the side of her face, turning pink in the rain.

'David . . . Go!' Ceridwen said.

David's arm jerked. 'She's never called me David before.'

Jessie pulled at him again and this time he followed her. The ground rose sharply, slippery with mud. Storm zigzagged in front of them, sniffing at the earth.

'I should have stayed a hare,' David muttered as a red flash lit up the trees behind them. 'Hares never have this kind of trouble. You become human, then you start to think like a human. You start caring about things, and it always ends in disaster.'

A tree fell over behind them with a crash that made Jessie jump. Her heart felt like it was about to burst out of her. Ceridwen shouted, and the shout turned into an animal cry of pain. Looking back, Jessie could see flashes of light, like fireworks through the trees. She slowed, but Storm ran back and nipped at her heels.

'I wish I'd never even heard of Abergavenny,' she said, breathless.

David caught up with her. 'If it helps, I'm glad you're here. If I have to be in mortal peril, I'd rather do it with a friend.' He clambered up a steep patch and turned back, holding out his hand. 'You don't seem very surprised by all this. Most humans refuse to believe in magic, even if it happens right in front of them.'

Jessie grasped his hand to pull herself up. 'I think if something is happening right in front of you it's a good idea to believe in it.' Besides, after seeing David turn into a hare and back she was prepared to believe anything was possible.

Storm ran around them, barking, as another flash of magic lit the sky.

'Don't worry,' Jessie said to him. 'They won't hurt you. I won't let them.'

They couldn't help by going back. They had to go on – they had to find the Hunt. It was the only way Storm would ever be safe.

They kept running, stumbling over the rough ground, until the slope levelled and they emerged from the trees on to a wide ridge where the wind howled in their faces. Jessie stopped, and rested her hands on her knees, panting for breath. Above them, the sky rolled with thick, black cloud. Jessie could just make out the town spread out between the mountains.

'Well, we're here,' she said. 'What do we do now?'

Storm growled like thunder. Straightening up, Jessie saw a red mass collect over the treetops and three shapes rise into it. *The professors.*

Jessie reached for David's hand, her insides churning. Ceridwen had failed. The professors were coming – and where was the Wild Hunt? Storm jumped up at her, pawing at the bottom of her coat.

'It's all right,' Jessie said. Her voice shook. 'I won't let them have you.'

'Neither will I,' David said fiercely. Jessie shot him a grateful smile and started to run along the ridge, looking about for anywhere they could hide. Nothing. There weren't even any trees up here, just rough jags of rock. The sky rumbled and an answering tremor shook the ground.

'You can stop running now,' a voice said behind them. It was Professor Utterby.

Jessie stumbled. David let out a low cry of dismay.

The three professors stepped on to the mountain ridge together. Nuffield and Ryston had lost their weapons, and all three of them were bleeding in places – that was something, at least. Professor Utterby leaned on his staff and held one hand inside his coat as if injured.

David started forward. 'What have you done with my aunt?' His whole body was shaking.

Professor Utterby smiled and drew his hand out from under his coat.

Jessie gasped. Storm barked and David swayed and stumbled.

Professor Utterby held a white hare by the back legs. It twitched feebly in his grasp, its amber eyes wide open but clouded and unseeing.

'Your aunt's magic isn't as strong as she likes to think,' Professor Utterby said carelessly. 'She really shouldn't have challenged us. It was three against one, after all.'

'Let her go,' David shouted. His face was white, his fists clenched.

'Gladly.' Professor Utterby tossed the hare's limp body into the grass. 'And, in exchange, you'll hand over the dog.'

David stood, tears running down his face with

the rain. *He'd agree.* He had to: he couldn't let his aunt die. He'd let the professors take Storm, and he'd blame himself forever for it. Jessie's ankle throbbed and she had a stitch in her side, but she barely felt the pain. The professors had won.

'She might even recover – in time,' Professor Nuffield said with a smile.

And then Jessie was angry. The professors didn't need to do this. They could take Storm now and there was nothing she or David could do to stop them. They just wanted David to admit his aunt had lost.

She bent to stroke Storm's wet coat with a trembling hand. 'Don't worry,' she said. 'It'll be all right.' It was the biggest lie she'd ever told. How could anything be all right after this?

Lightning split the sky right above her.

'You could still join us,' Professor Ryston said. 'Don't you want to know all the secrets of the world?'

Was he really that stupid?

'No,' Jessie said. 'I don't.' She wanted to be normal, to live with her mum and dad and Ben, and she didn't even care where they lived any more. She wanted to go to school, go to birthday parties, draw pictures of Storm playing in the garden and not have to worry about people trying to hurt him. Mum and Dad had split their family in half, but the professors were threatening to destroy everything.

The rage inside her compacted down to a single,

white-hot point. She stood up straight and faced the three of them. She knew she couldn't beat them – she'd just seen them defeat Ceridwen. All she could do was gain them a little time for David to do something clever, or for help to come. 'I am Jessica Price,' she said. 'Protector of my Friends and my Home. Professor Utterby, Professor Ryston, Professor Nuffield, by all the laws of magic, I challenge you.'

Everything stopped. Her words hung in the air like thunder. The professors stared at her, their mouths dropping open.

'Jessie, no!' David said, aghast.

Professor Utterby took a step back. 'You're challenging *us*? You and the puppy?'

Jessie hadn't thought to bring Storm into it, but she felt him pressing against her legs. She locked her knees to stop them trembling and nodded. 'Yes. Me and the puppy. The sorcerer's challenge, right? You can't do anything until you've accepted or surrendered.'

Professor Utterby laughed softly. 'I don't think so. Nuffield, get the dog.'

Ryston shook his head. 'Sorry. This is unorthodox, but she *has* challenged.'

'He's right,' Nuffield said.

Jessie's heart pounded.

'They'll kill you,' David whispered, his voice fierce.

'I know.' They didn't want to, though: she could see

the hesitation in their faces. It was the only thing that gave her hope.

Professor Utterby lowered his gaze. 'It appears we have no choice. Challenge—'

Then Storm howled.

CHAPTER 38

I am Storm of Odin and I am here.

His cry felt like a solid thing, crashing off stones and trees, echoing right up to the sky and back. He filled it with all his frustration, his rage at this confusing, broken world. The dog prison, the vet with her needles, the annoyance of cats. The obedience class where humans practised pretending they were in charge. He caught the scent of hare, the solid warmth of sheep and, with them, a faint but unmistakeable trace of dogs, horses and ancient magic.

He was a stormhound, a creature of the Otherworld. His heart beat with magic. And his tears . . .

He dropped his head, left Jessie's side and padded to where the white hare lay shivering in the grass. She would have killed him, but only because she didn't know any better. And she was David's family, not by blood but with ties far stronger than that. If she died, David would suffer, and Jessie with him.

'What's he doing?' Professor Utterby murmured.

Storm lay down next to Ceridwen, his howls

turning to broken whines. The rain drummed down harder than ever, pouring off his already soaked fur, streaming down his face. He thought about Jessie going back to the dog prison, choosing a dog that wasn't him. Maybe she'd even keep the silver food bowls, the same lead. She'd go on walks, and the new dog would sleep on her bed, curled at her feet.

I am Storm of Odin, stormhound of the Wild Hunt. He blinked, and two of the drops of water that ran down his face were not rain. They spilt in twin silver trails from his eyes and dripped on to the hare's body.

The hare shuddered. Lightning broke the sky and all the rocks around them heaved as if the mountain were about to split open.

'Stop him,' Nuffield said, his voice sharp with panic. Storm jumped back, snarling as Professor Utterby moved to grab him. Another flash of lightning. And, on the ground, white fur bristled, shifted and changed.

Ceridwen stood between Storm and the professors, whole again.

'The tears of a stormhound,' David breathed. 'They heal all injuries.'

He ran to Ceridwen, and she put an arm round his shoulders, gazing down at Storm. 'I never imagined anyone would shed tears for me,' she said. 'Let alone a stormhound. I may have been wrong about you.'

Yes, you were, Storm agreed.

'Of course you were wrong,' Jessie said. 'Storm

is the best dog in the world.'

Not a dog, Jessie. He raised his head to the sky and howled again.

'Excuse me,' Professor Utterby said, 'I hate to bring it up, but the child did challenge us.'

Then the sky parted overhead and thunder came charging over the mountain like the hooves of giant horses. The sky filled with howling: dozens of voices answering him. Storm felt himself swell with the sound.

I am Storm of Odin, hound of the Wild Hunt. I am here.

He turned and faced the figures emerging from the storm. Horses alighted on the brown earth, breathing out smoke and flame. Hounds rushed past, barking in a frenzy. And, at the head of them all, swinging his legs over his horse and jumping with a thump on to the storm-flattened grass, was a figure clad in grey armour. He stood taller than the horses, broad-shouldered and wild. His hair flowed out from beneath a bronze helmet. He held a spear that was as tall as he was. His left eye was dark as the hills, and, where his right eye should be, a livid scar spread across the empty socket.

Odin. The god of the storm.

Storm flattened himself to the grass. The Wild Hunt had returned.

CHAPTER 39

Jessie stared in amazement. Dogs surrounded her –
dogs so big their shoulders were level with hers, some
as black as midnight, others with long, pale coats
and red ears. And horses with crimson manes, their
breath steaming in the rain, hooves churning up mud
on the mountain ridge. And, in the middle of them
all, the man she'd seen in her dream. His armour was
patched and broken as if it had weathered a thousand
storms. His single eye burned with fierce light and the
ground trembled where he trod.

The three professors had turned completely white.
Ryston and Nuffield were trying to hide behind
Professor Utterby.

'Girl, we accept your challenge,' Utterby said
quickly. His face twitched in a nervous smile. 'Now
no one can touch us until we have fought.'

Ceridwen cast Jessie a frown. She seemed least
affected of them all by the sudden appearance of the
Wild Hunt.

'You challenged them?' she asked Jessie. 'By all the

powers of magic, whatever possessed you to do such a stupid thing?'

Jessie swallowed the lump in her throat. 'They were going to kill Storm.'

Storm stood up, and Jessie saw that he'd grown. He was almost as tall as she was now, his head level with her shoulder. Jessie ought to be afraid, but somehow she wasn't. The dogs and the horses, even the tall, one-eyed man, seemed familiar, and not just from her dreams.

Odin looked from Jessie to the professors and back. 'You were a brave child before, and you still are,' he said. 'If you have challenged, then you must follow it through and fight.'

Then he smiled, and handed Jessie his spear.

And Jessie remembered . . .

Baby brothers were boring, even on holiday.

Especially on holiday. Mum and Dad had no time to play. All they wanted to do was feed the baby, change the baby's clothes, bath the baby. Everything was about the baby, and Jessie was starting to wish Ben had never arrived in their house.

Now it was raining and she wasn't even allowed to go in the garden. She hated this silly little house, and she hated being a big sister. Why should Ben get everything, just because he was smaller?

The front window had a wide, wooden seat,

and she knelt there with her face against the glass, watching the rain. Maybe, if it rained hard enough, this house would be washed away and they could all go home.

The sky outside grumbled as if agreeing with her. Then Jessie saw something. As the thunder rolled, a quick flash of light lit the clouds and she thought she saw horses.

'Look,' she said. But Mum was asleep, her head nodding on her chest, and Dad wasn't there at all. Jessie slid down from the seat and padded out to the staircase. She heard his voice, singing to the baby.

'Horses,' she said.

Dad paused. 'That's nice. Be a good girl.'

But she wanted to see the horses. She looked up at the front door, then stood on tiptoe and grasped the handle. It was almost too high to reach, but she just managed it. The door swung inwards, almost knocking her off her feet. Silly door. Jessie picked up Mum's umbrella – she knew you needed umbrellas in the rain – and, trailing it behind her, she walked out uncertainly into the storm.

She couldn't see the horses any more. Where had they gone? She marched to the garden gate and, because it was open, she went through, crossed the lane outside and squeezed through a gap in the hedge into the field beyond. Her umbrella snagged on the hedge and she left it there. She saw sheep in the next field, and a great tree, bigger than anything she'd ever seen before. Jessie started towards it.

Lightning flashed and she fell down, too surprised to cry. Then a horse landed right in front of her, almost as if it had fallen from the sky. Another one followed, and another. Dogs too. Jessie tried to hug the legs of one of them. It licked her face and she giggled.

A tall man got down from a horse. He wore a funny-looking helmet with horns and he only had one eye.

'Poor face,' Jessie said.

The man bent his knees until his face was only just above hers. 'You shouldn't be out here, little one.' His voice was deep as thunder. 'Where have you come from?'

Jessie pointed back across the field. 'I came to see the horses.'

The horses were beautiful, but frightening too. Something told Jessie they shouldn't be out here either.

'You're too big,' she said. 'Go away. Go home.'

The big man gave a rumble of laughter. 'You're a brave child.' He set her on his horse and led her across the grass to the tree. Jessie clung on, rain running into her open mouth, too frightened, too fascinated, to cry.

'Stay here,' the man said, putting her down under

the tree. 'You'll be safe.' He looked into her face, his single eye holding her gaze. 'You have a baby brother,' he said softly. 'You should protect him. The people you love are your home. As you grow, you'll understand that.'

Then he called to the riders and the dogs, and they raced across the field and back into the sky. Jessie stood and watched, until there was another flash of lightning and they vanished.

Moments later, she heard Dad shouting her name.

'Jessie,' David said, shaking her arm. Jessie blinked and wiped her hands over her face.

'I really did go outside to see the horses,' she said. She turned to the one-eyed man. 'I saw them. I saw you.'

He nodded gravely. 'Few mortals do. You had a touch of magic to you even then, I think. And now it is up to you. This is your home – protect it.'

Her home. Jessie glanced to either side at David and Storm. David grinned nervously and Storm bared his teeth and growled. In a moment he was almost as big as the other dogs that milled about the mountain peak. He sat down, bared his teeth and growled.

Utterby stepped back. 'Maybe I was too hasty . . .'

Odin's spear buzzed in Jessie's hand. She gripped it firmly, thinking of Mum and Dad and Ben, the new house, her school, Prisha who'd invited her to a party . . . even Mrs Williams next door. 'You don't belong here,' she said slowly. 'You're not taking Storm – you're not taking anything. Go away.'

Professor Utterby aimed his staff at her, then he seemed to change his mind, grabbed something out of his pocket with his left hand and threw it. White crystals stung her eyes. *Salt.*

'Storm, look out!' Jessie said, remembering the chemistry class. Storm shook himself as the first crystals burst into flame.

'It's a shame you wouldn't let us teach you,' Professor Utterby said. 'You have talent. Still, there are plenty of other people in the world who do want to learn. We'll find them.'

He threw another handful of salt. Little fires flickered all around, most of them going out quickly in the rain. Jessie stepped back, suddenly uncertain. Who did she think she was, challenging the professors?

Storm nudged her. *You can do this.*

She wasn't sure whether the thought came from Storm or from herself, but she felt warmth spread through her.

Professor Utterby thumped his staff on the ground and his gaze flicked to Ryston and Nuffield on either side of him. 'On the count of three,' he said. 'One, two . . .'

His staff blazed with magical light. Jessie swung Odin's spear without thinking. Lightning and earthfire met in a crash that made the mountain tremble. Jessie shouted, but kept hold of Odin's staff, steadying it in both hands as light poured out of it. Every hair on her body seemed to be standing on end.

"I am Jessie Price," a voice cried – her own voice, though she barely recognized it. "I am Lightning Bug!"

The light spread, swallowing up the professors, and then, just as suddenly, it blinked out of existence. Jessie blinked in the sudden gloom.

Professor Utterby squeaked. It was the only sound he could make, seeing as he'd just been turned into a mouse. Nuffield and Ryston, cowering behind him, turned to run, but they too shrank as they fled, leaving their clothes in heaps and scuttling away squealing into the long grass. A few of the hounds looked as if they were about to give chase, but a sharp word from Odin stopped them.

The spear fell from Jessie's hand. Storm sat down beside her while she stood shaking, staring at the three soggy heaps of clothes on the ground.

'Well done,' Ceridwen said.

'Well done? I . . . I just . . .' *I used magic. It was like lightning inside me. I turned three men into mice.*

'You did nothing,' Odin said. 'It was my spear, my power. They'll revert back to their human forms in time. A few weeks, maybe a few months. This might teach them not to meddle with powers that are beyond their control.' He bent to scoop up his spear.

237

'You have a spark of magic in you, child. Guard it well. And now, farewell. Storm of Odin, come.'

He turned back to his horse, calling to the other riders and the dogs. Storm's tail thumped the ground and he stood up and shook himself.

This was it: time to say goodbye.

Jessie's eyes filled with tears. 'Go,' she said. 'It's all right. I'll be all right. You have to go.'

Storm licked her cheek and turned his head away from her. Jessie closed her eyes so she wouldn't see the moment he left.

'Come!' Odin commanded.

But then David was shaking her, pulling her through the crush of hounds and horses after Odin.

'Wait,' David said. 'Storm, stay! Odin, sir, you can't do this. You have to let Storm choose.'

CHAPTER 40

Storm paused amid the impatient hounds and horses as Odin prepared to mount his steed and ride off into the sky. Even as Storm felt the muscles in his legs shift and bunch, ready to take him in one great leap off this world, he heard the Not-Boy's voice calling to him to stay and, he turned back.

I am Storm of Odin, hound of the Wild Hunt. Who do you think you are, telling me to stay?

Odin rested one hand on his horse's saddle. 'Let him choose?' His voice rumbled like thunder. 'There *is* no choice. Storm of Odin is a stormhound, not a mortal dog to be commanded by humans. He belongs with the Hunt and nowhere else. You cannot be two things.'

'Why not?' the Not-Boy asked. He pushed forward another step, his gaze flicking nervously over the prowling hounds. 'I'm a hare and a boy. And Jessie has two homes. If she can have two homes and I can be two things, why can't Storm?'

Lightning flashed, fainter and further away this time.

Odin shook his head. 'The world isn't like that.'

But he sounded slightly uncertain.

Ceridwen laughed. 'Actually, the world is *exactly* like that.' She made her way through the hunters and put her hand on the Not-Boy's shoulder. 'David is right: people are a lot messier than you'd like to think, and so are most things.' Her gaze strayed to Storm again.

Storm wagged his tail – she had a point. Not long ago, he'd thought she was a foul sorceress who wanted to kill him, but it turned out she wasn't.

The Not-Boy grinned. 'Does this mean you'll let me do more magic?'

Ceridwen gave him a pretend glare. 'No. But it does mean we might stay on here for a while so you can keep going to school. It won't hurt to have a base of operations. Somewhere to call home while we're saving the world,' she added with a faint smile.

The Not-Boy's face lit up. Storm sniffed his hand.

You still stink of hare, but you're all right. I might miss you. He would, too, just like he'd miss Jessie and Ben and their ridiculously small house.

'The storm is moving on,' Odin said, 'and we must follow.' But instead of getting up on to his horse he thrust his spear into the ground and walked back to where Storm was waiting, then crouched down low so that he was looking straight into Storm's eyes.

Storm shivered. Odin's face was stern and old –

far older than the mortal world – and his single eye glinted like firelight.

'Very well,' he said softly. 'Choose, Storm of Odin. Return to the Hunt, leave your human friends and be a stormhound again. Or stay here. In this world, you will always look like a mortal dog. You will live outside of my protection. I cannot say what will happen to you, or promise when we will next return. It may be years. It may be never.'

His words burned into Storm's heart. Storm swished his tail, feeling its tip bat against Jessie's legs. The strange empty space was back and he knew what that emptiness was: the longing for home. It didn't make sense. Ever since he'd fallen into this world, all he'd wanted was to escape and return to the Hunt where he belonged, so why did the emptiness still bother him?

All around, the huntsmen were mounting their horses, eager to take flight. Jessie put her arms around Storm's neck and buried her face in his coat.

'Go, Storm,' she said, her voice muffled. She let go of him and stepped back. Her eyes were full of tears, but she wiped them away. 'Go home.'

She smelled the same as when they'd first met – sharp as lightning. Storm had been so small then, and now he was almost the same height as her. Tall enough that she could climb on his back and ride on him.

Storm shook himself, padded across to Odin, sat down and let out a sigh.

I am Storm of Odin and I have chosen.

Then he walked back to Jessie, lay down in front of her and nudged at her, urging her on to his back.

She laughed through her tears. 'I can't, Storm. I wish I could, but I can't go with you. I belong here.'

All this talk about belonging is wrong, Storm thought. *You don't belong to a place, you belong to yourself, and to the people you love.*

Storm nudged at Jessie again.

'He's not inviting you to hunt,' Odin said gravely. 'He wants to carry you home.' He bent and placed one hand on Storm's head. 'You've chosen well,' he said.

'No!' Jessie said, understanding at last. Her lightning-sharp scent flared even stronger, filling the whole sky. Her scent was even in Storm's eyes now, clouding them so that he saw Odin in a blur. Jessie's face was wet too.

'It's not your decision to make, mortal child,' Odin said. 'Get on his back. Storm, run with us this last time. We will take you home.' He stood up, his hand slipping away from Storm's head. 'Farewell, hound of the Wild Hunt.'

'Go,' Ceridwen said. 'We'll see you back in town.'

Tears dripped into Storm's coat as Jessie clambered up on to his back and clung on.

Storm already felt himself becoming smaller. He

242

tensed, drew back and jumped, and the whole Hunt leaped into the sky with him. Their cries echoed from mountain to mountain, louder than thunder.

He was Storm of Odin, running through the sky with thunderclouds around him. He was Storm of Odin, with the weight of a human child on his back and the freedom of the sky beneath his feet.

He was Storm of Odin, seeing familiar roofs beneath him, dipping gently out of the sky . . .

No, not straight home. There was something else he needed to do first. A stormhound always keeps his word. The Hunt understood and let him lead, down from the sky to a white building with a sign that read: *Abergavenny Dog Rescue Centre*.

Hounds and horses shimmered as they passed silently through the roof. They landed inside between the two rows of wire cells where dogs, suddenly awake, sat up and barked.

The white terrier's cell was empty. Gone to a new home, no doubt. Storm would have to look out for him. But for now he stopped outside the cell where the old female dog lay.

I have returned, Storm of Odin said. *As I promised.*

So you have, the female dog replied. *And?*

And Odin has a space for a new dog. If you want it.

He tugged the wire door of her cell open. Odin

placed his spear on the old dog's back and she grew, becoming young again, and she leaped into the sky with the others.

He was Storm of Odin, following the baying hounds, falling behind now, but not minding because, just a short distance on, a familiar garden waited, and a tabby cat hissed and fled over the fence with a flick of her tail.

He was Storm of Odin, shrinking back to his puppy size as the house door opened and Jessie's dad, the Mum-Person, and Ben ran out.

He was Storm, nudging Jessie into their arms, and listening as they all babbled in the way that humans did.

For a moment, Storm remembered what he'd lost, and the vast, empty space opened inside him again, dark as the sky. But then he heard the fading howls in the night, and a new voice among them, the voice of an old dog who was remembering how to run.

Jessie picked him up and buried her face in his fur. 'It's good to be home,' she said.

Storm wriggled against her.

He was Storm, Jessie's dog, and the promise of home was bright and warm, filling the empty space inside him until he forgot it was ever there.

SOME MONTHS LATER

'Dad, I'm home,' Jessie shouted. 'Can David stay for dinner?'

'If he wants to.' Dad came out into the hall wearing an apron. 'I had a go at making cake. I thought we should celebrate the end of your first term in school. It's not the world's best cake, I'm afraid – it came out a bit wonky.'

'Then it'll be perfect,' Jessie said. The first term had been a bit wonky, but it was getting better. They'd made new friends, Ben had joined his school football team and Mum still phoned every day.

'Can you help Ben pack later?' Dad asked. 'He's only going to London for a week, but he wants to take everything. We don't have that many suitcases.'

Ben was going to Mum's for Christmas: his first full week with her in the new flat. Then, when he came home, Jessie would go for New Year. It wasn't ideal, but she was looking forward to it. It'd be odd not being all together for Christmas, though.

'What are you doing for Christmas?' she asked David.

He helped himself to cake. 'I don't know. We've never really celebrated it before. But Auntie Ceridwen said I can have a tree. As long as I decorate it myself and I don't mind leaving it behind if we have to move on in a hurry.'

There'd been no word of the professors since that night in September. The *Abergavenny Chronicle* had printed an article about their strange disappearance. The strangest thing, they said, was that the professors were on secondment from Bangor University but no one at Bangor had ever heard of them. There must have been an administrative mix-up.

Jessie cut a slice of cake and licked the icing off. It might look wonky but it tasted good. 'Let's go upstairs,' she said. Storm had taken to sleeping on her bed in the day, and after numerous attempts to keep him out of the room, Dad had given up and let him do it.

'Auntie Ceridwen thinks the professors will turn up again sometime,' David said, following her up the stairs, 'or something else will happen. But she's getting less fussy. Last night she said she'd decided we can allow small infractions of the rules and only respond to major emergencies. Then she won't have to work so hard, and I might even get some homework done on time.'

Jessie doubted that. David was still consistently late with everything.

'What does she mean by "small infractions"?' she asked.

David shrugged. 'Anything she decides to ignore, I guess. She seems to be making the rules up as she goes along, these days.'

He opened the bedroom door and Jessie looked up at the ceiling with a sigh. Storm barked at her happily, his tail hitting the lightbulb and making it sway from side to side.

'Storm,' Jessie said, 'what have I told you about flying in the house?'

ACKNOWLEDGEMENTS

I began writing this book on a trip to Abergavenny. Wales is a land full of legend and the small town, surrounded by mountains, seemed the perfect place for something magical to happen. I invented the high school and the dog rescue centre but you'll find all the other places if you visit. In fact, you'll find two Mount Skirrids: big and little. Big Skirrid, where Storm fell, really does have a chunk missing. Legend says the devil stamped his foot on it but I like to think the Wild Hunt landed there and broke it.

I am indebted to many, many people, as always.

My 'book family' at Macmillan Children's – the legendary Lucy Pearse, along with Tracey, Nick, Sam, Venetia, Alyx, Sabina, Jess, Emma and Kat, for bringing Storm's adventure magnificently to life.

My agent Gemma, who must have a touch of Otherworldly magic to make her so special.

My writing friends for their help and encouragement. Everyone I have thanked before, you are all thanked again! Especially Abigail Tanner for suggesting the sheep and Jo Thomas for the Abergavenny road trip.

Thank you, Vee Griffiths for knitting me my very own super-cute stormhound puppy and for being such a solid, good friend to so many people.

A Literature Wales Writer's Bursary supported by the National Lottery through the Arts Council of Wales was received to develop this book. Diolch yn fawr i chi gyd!

ABOUT THE AUTHOR

Claire Fayers was born and brought up in South Wales. Having studied English at Canterbury Christ Church University, she built a successful career writing short stories for women's magazines until the lure of magic became too much and she wrote *The Accidental Pirates: Voyage to Magical North*. It was selected for Waterstones Book of the Month, won the Beano Book of the Year 2017 and was shortlisted for the FCBG Children's Book Award 2016.

Claire is also the author of its sequel, *The Accidental Pirates: Journey to Dragon Island*, and *Mirror Magic*. When she's not writing, you'll find Claire at her allotment.

HAVE YOU READ

THE ACCIDENTAL PIRATES
VOYAGE TO MAGICAL NORTH

CLAIRE FAYERS

THE ACCIDENTAL PIRATES
JOURNEY TO DRAGON ISLAND

CLAIRE FAYERS

'EXCITING, CLEVER AND MAGICAL – THE PERFECT RECIPE FOR ADVENTURE'
ROBIN STEVENS

'EXCITING, CLEVER AND MAGICAL – THE PERFECT RECIPE FOR ADVENTURE'
ROBIN STEVENS

MIRROR MAGIC

CLAIRE FAYERS
AUTHOR OF THE ACCIDENTAL PIRATES